Humble Glory

Dodge Merrin

eBook Edition ISBN-13: 979-8-9909079-0-4

Paperback ISBN-13: 979-8-9909079-1-1

Cover design by Mirko Fermani

<u>Content Warning:</u> *This book contains depictions of violence with some graphic descriptions of bleeding, broken bones, and other injuries.*

Contents

Chapter One

A Man Alone

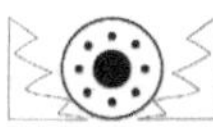

Darkness shrouded the path through the thick forest, but the dirt path beneath the warrior's sandaled feet was bare and free from any foliage, confirming that his target must be nearby. No one else was likely to be coming and going this deep in The Great Forest.

He walked quickly with a short sword in his right hand. All of his senses were tuned to the world around him, yet he saw nothing but the shadowy shapes of trees and spiny underbrush, heard only birdsong and small creatures scampering across fallen leaves, and his nostrils detected no more than the smell of damp earth moistened by the morning dew.

The stories of attacks upon travelers on the nearby road revealed this to be the latest hunting ground of the bandits plaguing the countryside these past months. The army normally resolved such matters with brutal efficiency, but this group was wily enough to move out of a region before their base camp could be located, then set up in another area seemingly chosen at random. Unable to stretch its standing resources to cover its entire territory, especially given the rumors of trouble brewing at the northern and eastern borders, the senate of the great Naeran Republic had placed a large bounty on the head of the group's leader in the hope his death or capture would scatter the rest.

When Raldus Velix, a warrior of Stoneforge trained from childhood to be among the best fighters in all the known lands, heard of this bounty, he knew this was the opportunity which he'd long sought. For over two years now, since completing his training at age eighteen, he'd wandered the land from the great cities to humble towns looking to make a name for himself. Yet in all that time, he'd barely earned enough pay to stay fed and equipped for battle.

Over his beige tunic, he wore a brown leather breastplate and cingulum, which was a belt with leather strips hanging from it to cover his upper legs. Leather bracers covered his forearms, but his shins were bare save for the leather straps of his sandals which wrapped around up to his knees. All of it was old and mismatched, but well-oiled and cinched tight.

The blade of the sword in his right hand matched the length of his arm and shined even in the low light, while his left hand remained empty but was equally ready to strike. His means may be small, but his equipment always came first.

He'd spent the previous night in that armor sitting braced against the opposite side of a tree several paces beside the path he now traveled, sword in hand and no fire to warm him. He sensed his quarry was near, but nothing had awoken him until the birds welcomed the new day with their songs. All he did upon waking was to stand and shake off the chill which had seeped into his bones during the night, and when he was sure no enemies were nearby, he'd propped the sword against the tree long enough to stretch his tight muscles and check the fittings on his armor, then relieved himself before reclaiming the sword and returning to the path.

There was no way to know for sure how much time had passed with the sun hidden above the dense canopy, but it felt like at least two or three hours until at last a light appeared ahead, growing in time with his pace to soon reveal a gap in the trees. He slowed long enough to allow his eyes to adjust as he stepped into a clearing, then he continued forward in a slight crouch while turning in a circle as he walked.

The grass and flowers rustled as a slight breeze blew from the east, carrying with it the scent of decomposing leaves, but mixed in with the earthy smell was another that did not belong. He breathed deep without disrupting his pace, and identified the extra odor as that of human sweat and grime, telling him someone was hiding among the trees.

Another small gust revealed that the smell was far stronger than it should be at this distance, which could only mean there was more than one potential enemy waiting to ambush him. Such information would cause a lesser man to turn back, but he kept going, his lips pulling back into a tight smile.

This might actually prove to be a challenge for once.

He had crossed almost halfway when a shout from the treeline drew his gaze and he froze as several armed men broke out and ran toward him, silent save for the sound of their rapid footsteps. Each one was dressed differently, from wearing nothing but a half-tunic to cover their genitals to sets of armor even more mismatched than his own, and certainly less maintained. Their weapons were equally disparate with a variety of swords, clubs, and axes, plus a few of them even had shields from the smallish round ones favored by the tribes in bordering lands to the large rectangular style used by the Naeran army.

The warrior resumed his slow turn as over a dozen of them came from all sides and surrounded him, but he made no move to attack or flee.

"What's this? A lost pup wandering in the woods?" a harsh voice accused. A large man with brown hair hanging over his ears and a scraggly beard covering his face stepped out from the others as they all chuckled at his little joke. The warrior stood to his own imposing, yet somewhat shorter, height to deliver his answer.

"My name is Raldus Velix and you, Tallio Atroni, are coming with me."

This time the laughter was much louder and the leader joined in as the loudest of them all.

"I don't go anywhere I don't want, boy."

"I did not ask if it was what you wanted."

"Do you wish to die, wretch?" the bandit threatened, but all Raldus did was smile wide.

"Let me at 'im, boss!" a particularly ugly man, his saggy chest and gut darkened with grime on full display, requested.

"He's all yours."

The man roared in challenge, banged his axe on his shield twice, then charged his target while shouting as loud as possible. Raldus calmly waited for him to close the distance before darting to the right and sticking out his foot to trip his attacker. As the man fell, he grabbed his shield to hold him up long enough to stab him through the heart from the back, then swiftly pulled off the shield and slid his own arm through the straps.

Most of the man's companions stared at the scene in shock, but their leader's reaction was one of raucous laughter.

"Looks like you're not so dumb," he remarked, which he followed up with an irritated look at his men and asking, "What are you waiting for? Kill 'im!"

There was a brief hesitation, but then two ran in screaming, only to end up joining their comrade on the ground within seconds.

"Are you just going to keep lining up for 'im? Are all you too dull to take out one fool!"

This time one ran up from behind Raldus, but he still heard the man coming and spun around while crouching to slash him across both legs. Two more ran in, forcing him to block one with the shield while dodging the other.

Before he could counter, three more entered the fray and his world dissolved into dodging and blocking attacks with counterstrikes few and far between.

Then a hammer smashed into his shield, and he cried out in pain as it shattered and he stumbled back with left arm hugging his chest.

"About time! Now end it!"

A younger bandit, emboldened by the warrior's injury, leapt toward him holding a mace in both hands and raised for an overhead strike, but Raldus' sword slashed across his throat while still in the air and he crumpled to the ground gasping for air with blood streaming through his desperately clutching fingers.

A strike from behind drove Raldus to the ground, after which a foot stomped his right wrist and his sword wrested from his grip. He tried to stand up and shoulder the bandit off him, but that ambition was ended with a swift kick to his side.

More kicks than could be counted rained down on him, leaving him no room to fight back, and his world gradually turned dark.

The bandit leader chuckled as he strolled past the men who were bent over gasping for air. He stood over the interloper's body, smiling as he savored the moment, then leaned over and picked up the sword which still lay in the short brown grass nearby.

"Nice sword. Wonder who he killed for it. Eh, who cares, it's mine now," he remarked after tearing off the tunic sleeve of his nearest man to wipe off the dirt and blood.

He walked past the group while holding up the sword to admire it in the light and finally told them to help themselves to the rest.

The others set to work on the body, their earlier fatigue forgotten as they stripped off the armor and searched for any other gear he might have been carrying. Those who couldn't get to that corpse set to work on their fallen comrades to pilfer their gear without hesitation or remorse.

"Boss!" someone suddenly called out, and Tallio turned back to see those around the young fool standing back in shock.

Curious, he lowered the sword to his side and sauntered up to see them staring at a tattoo on the youth's outer right forearm just above his bracer. The black ink was marred by streaks of blood, but the symbol of a round shield between two cliffs was still recognizable.

"Stoneforge," someone gasped.

"Not even one of the best fighters in the world can beat us!" Tallio declared as he raised his arms high, causing the nearest man to lean back to avoid losing an eye.

He expected cheers, but got whispers instead, so he dropped his arms and glared at his men with disgust.

"What's the matter with you? He's dead. We're alive. Now everyone will fear us!"

"But..."

"He's right! We killed 'im! No one can stop us!"

Now most of them had the heart to cheer as pride swelled in Tallio's chest, lifting his chin as he grinned at his men.

"That's better. Now finish up. We have work to do," he commanded, then started walking away again.

"Should we cut it off as proof? Nobody would be fool enough to not give us what we want if we show them that."

"No, leave it. Our story will be good enough, and anyone who sees the body will also tell the tale. Now move it!"

Pain wracked Raldus' body with every movement, and he labored to breathe as he pulled himself forward by his right hand with his left arm dragging at his side. The taste of metal filled his mouth, and spitting out the blood every few seconds did little to lessen it.

He did not stop.

Rocks, sticks, and other debris scratched and cut his exposed skin as his tunic hung off him in shreds; he struggled to raise his head to look for obstacles, and bugs crawled across him, sensing an easy meal.

None of this deterred him.

He refused to die this way. His end would not come at the hands of a bunch of thugs. This forest would not be his final resting place, lost and forgotten for all time, nothing but another nameless skeleton picked over by scavenging beasts.

"Not this way," he grunted as he dug his fingers into the soft dirt and pulled. His vision blurred and darkened, and his face fell to the ground. It was soft and called him to rest, even if only for a little while.

"No."

His voice was scarcely a whisper. He tried to reach out again, but his arm would not move. Everything was growing numb, and even the pain was fading away.

I never fail. Never.

"Do what you can for him," Abbot Jerald directed after the teenage girl had finished examining the many wounds of the young man a hunter had found near their wall.

"I will tend to his needs for as long as he has them," Ariela promised as she dipped a cloth in the bucket of water beside her and began wiping off the dirt and dried blood.

"We would care for him ourselves, but you have more experience in such matters from helping when a farmer is injured," Jerald offered, and her response was a simple nod.

It was difficult to believe the young man was still alive in this condition, and impossible to hope he would recover. Everyone could see the cuts and bruises covering his naked body as he lay on the bed, but the girl had also reported finding three broken ribs, a shattered right wrist, and a broken left arm.

After helping carry the man to the monastery for treatment, the hunter had returned to where he found the lad and followed the trail of blood and disturbed ground to discover he had crawled for over a mile after fighting multiple attackers, the looted bodies of those he'd killed still lying in the clearing where it happened. The force of will in this man barely out of his teen years must be incredible.

"What is this?" Ariela questioned as she held up the man's right arm. On the forearm, amidst the scratches and bruises, was a black ink tattoo of a circle between two slanted, jagged lines.

"The mark of his creed."

He had heard of this symbol before, and the people who wore it, but didn't know that much about them other than their way was one of violence.

There were other duties for him to attend, so he turned to leave but stopped to address the young man in gray robes standing beside the door.

"He is to be watched at all times. Do not leave her alone with him."

The man screamed again as Ariela pressed the cool, damp cloth to his forehead and whispered to him, her soothing tone of greater importance than any words. It seemed to do little good as he continued to strain against the ropes holding him to the bed while railing against unseen terrors.

This was his second night under her care, and the fever which had taken hold on the first showed no signs of letting up. She hadn't wanted to restrain him in fear of causing more pain, especially given his broken wrist and arm, but the monks had insisted out of concern for her safety.

"You can't defeat me! Nobody can defeat me!" he shouted at the ceiling, his eyes wide but unseeing.

"Shh. You are safe here. No one is trying to hurt you."

"That means nothing! Nothing!"

"Be still. You must calm yourself," she insisted, but he only screamed and threw himself backward into the bed.

After her mother's death when she was but a little girl, she had assumed the responsibility of looking after her household while the men worked the fields. The other women of the community helped as needed and taught her many things, and experience taught her the rest.

In her eighteen years of life, she had provided care for the sick or injured many times, including one man trampled by a horse and who inevitably succumbed to his injuries. It was never easy to be near someone when they were suffering, especially when they seemed sure to die, but she never lost the will to do everything in her power to cure and comfort them.

She began softly singing a hymn as she refreshed the cloth in the bucket of water on the floor to her right, then used it to wipe the sweat from his face. Even if he couldn't understand her words, she hoped that the sound of her voice would at least bring him a measure of peace.

It was all she could do.

Chapter Two

When A Man Falls

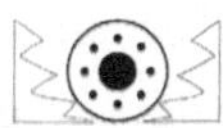

Waking felt like climbing out of a deep, dark well with a boulder strapped to his back, but Raldus forced open his eyes to the sight of candlelight dancing on a wooden ceiling. He slowly turned his head, wincing as pain shot through the numbness weighing him down, and in so doing discovered a young woman standing over him wringing out a cloth.

"Who...?" he managed to croak before his voice gave out.

"Do not fear," she reassured him as she placed the cool cloth on his forehead.

"Where?"

"Safe."

"What?"

"You are hurt, and have been delirious with fever for three days. Rest easy."

Sleep began to take hold once more, but he tensed his jaw to fight it off, as he needed to know more. Before he could speak again, a middle-aged balding man in gray robes entered and told the girl to leave.

She obeyed without question, so Raldus attempted to question the newcomer.

"Your questions can wait. Go back to sleep," the man ordered, then left without awaiting a response.

The warrior attempted to get up, but his stiff muscles resisted and he soon found himself drifting off to sleep.

A single candle and the coals on the hearth were all that lit the modest kitchen in Ariela's humble home with nothing but darkness to be seen through the small gap between shutter flaps blocking the window. She had already placed the bread and cheese on the table while a ceramic pot full of beans still hung on a hook over the hearth, the lid of which she now removed so she could stir them and ensure they would be ready for when her father Imri and brother Tobias woke before too long.

She would complete her chores, no matter how tired she may be from any amount of other work that came her way.

The others got up right before dawn, and the two of them rinsed their hands and faces using a bucket of water in the corner drawn from the town well before dusk the previous evening. Imri went first, and Tobias followed to splash away the last vestiges of sleep while their father took the linen towel from the nearby wall hook to dry himself, after which the teenage boy used the same towel before leaving it on the counter.

When that was done, they all took their breakfast at the wood table of four wide boards on rectangular legs in the kitchen, saying very little as there was nothing to be said. Another day of labor awaited them all, and each knew what they had to do.

Her father and younger brother finished eating and headed to work when the sky was starting to lighten, leaving her to clean up, which she did after opening the shutters and without complaint. By the time all was in order and she left the house to attend her duties at the monastery, the sky was lit bright blue by the sun now over the horizon, and the cows were lowing in the fields while birds sang their dawn greetings.

She breathed deep of the early spring air, feeling quite warm in her beige linen dress and red woolen shawl, refreshing herself in the new day as she walked the stone path from the houses to the monastery complex on the hill overlooking the town.

Morning light streaming through the slats of a shuttered window woke Raldus, and after allowing himself a quiet groan of discontent, he slowly sat up in the bed, using only his right forearm to prop himself up since the left one was bandaged across his chest. A man, dressed similar to the one from the previous night but younger and with a full head of short black hair, entered and attempted to gently push him back down while insisting he still needed to rest.

"Get away from me!" the warrior growled as he shrugged the hands away from his shoulders.

"You are not yet healed," the man stammered as he stood there wide-eyed.

"I know what I'm doing!" Raldus responded, his voice rising. The flustered man, who couldn't be more than a few years older than his charge, attempted to say something else, but his mouth just kept opening and closing without sound until he finally fled from the room, red-faced.

It took a bit of time, but he managed to sit up in the bed to swing his legs around and stand up, all the while clenching his jaw against the pain wracking every part of his body. Bandages wrapped his entire torso in addition to the ones holding his left arm to his chest, and even more were wrapped so tightly around his right forearm and hand that he couldn't move it at the wrist or flex the fingers. Scabbed cuts and purplish bruises covered his bare legs, and he could only guess at the state of his face.

He spotted a fresh loincloth and his tunic hanging on the back of a solitary chair, so he donned both as quickly as he could. When he looked down at the beige tunic, he noticed at least three places where someone had so expertly sewn up tears that the stitches were almost invisible.

Why anyone would go through the trouble of not only tending his wounds but also fixing his clothes was beyond his reasoning, but he put the confusion out of his mind and began searching for his equipment. When he couldn't find either armor or weapons in the small room, his suspicion increased, and he grew warm from the anger manifesting to match it.

Raised voices greeted Ariela as she approached the stranger's room, and she quickened her pace in concern. After turning the corner into the hall, she spotted Brother Melcor standing in the doorway to block their guest from exiting the room.

"I will not be held captive!" the stranger shouted. He appeared ready to strike the exasperated monk, despite needing to prop himself up on the chair to keep standing and having only limited use of only one arm, but he calmed down when he saw her coming.

"I need to check your bandages," she addressed him calmly, without commenting on the argument. Melcor looked unsure for a moment, but then the stranger nodded his consent and sat down on the edge of the bed, so the monk let her in.

"You were here last night," the outsider commented after she removed his tunic and began working on the bandages covering his torso. Her only reply was a brief nod, and he didn't say anything else.

He watched her, his green eyes focused on her face as she tended his wounds. This made her a bit uncomfortable, but there was no hostility there, so she just ignored him and kept her attention on what she was doing.

Then his gaze darted to the door, and a moment later, she heard a deep voice telling Melcor to wait outside. She recognized the voice as belonging to Jerald, the head of the monastery, and continued working.

"What is your name?" Jerald demanded of the stranger.

"Raldus Velix."

"Do you know where you are? Who we are?"

The answer was a shake of the head to say no.

"What business does Stoneforge have in the area?"

"Do you always question guests in this manner?"

"We don't have many guests here. We prefer to keep to ourselves. What is your business here?"

"You know what I do," Raldus remarked as he held up and presented his right forearm to the abbot. A bandage currently covered it because of the broken wrist and cuts, but Ariela had seen the tattoo during his initial care and pointed it out to the monks. She didn't know what it meant, but evidently Jerald did.

"Why are you here?"

"I might be able to answer that if you told me who you are and what this place is!" Raldus shot back.

Both were silent for a time, and although she didn't look up at them, Ariela easily imagined that they were both staring each other down. Jerald was accustomed to being obeyed, but this man did not fear or respect him.

"Please lie down," Ariela spoke up.

His first response was to stare at her as if he'd forgotten she was even there.

"No," he said a moment later.

"I need to clean the wounds on your legs," she insisted, but he did nothing.

"She is the only reason you are still alive. For three days, she cared for you while you thrashed and screamed at nothing," Jerald revealed, his tone stern. The man's features softened as he looked into her eyes, and he finally lay down and allowed her to continue.

"We are an order of monks. This is our monastery," Jerald explained, ending their standoff.

"You don't look like any priests I've ever seen."

"We keep to ourselves."

"This is in the great forest?"

She didn't see Jerald nod, but saw in Raldus' expression that he had answered thusly.

"I was hunting a bandit who has been hiding nearby. I didn't even know you were here and don't care now that I do. All I want is to get out of here."

"We don't like having outsiders here, but we won't deny someone in need. You can stay until you are healed, but you will be watched at all times," Jerald decreed, then left without another word.

Raldus nearly jumped out of the bed to go give that man a piece of his mind, but a sharp pain in his right shin stopped him and he grit his teeth to keep from crying out.

"Sorry," his caretaker apologized without slowing.

As he watched her, his anger subsided upon seeing she was quite tired, but not allowing it to affect her work or attitude. He couldn't help but wonder why she would work so hard to help someone whom she'd never met and her people didn't even want around. Why would that old man even allow it if they hated outsiders so much?

"I'm finished. The infection is almost gone and you are starting to heal," she concluded as she pulled the blanket over him. Then she gathered her things and left as another monk was bringing in a tray holding a bowl of soup and a cup of water. He set it down on the bed, sat in the chair vacated by the girl, and picked up the bowl before leaning toward Raldus.

"I don't need you to feed me," Raldus spat. The monk shrugged in response, set the bowl back down, and left.

He propped himself up well enough to eat and drink, then settled back down and drifted off to sleep once again.

"So he's awake," Keid commented as the abbot came down the hall toward him from the room where they had sequestered the stranger.

"Yes," Jerald responded as he walked past, clearly not wanting to talk, but the monk fell into step beside him anyway.

"Is he going to live, after all?"

"It appears that way."

"That can be nothing short of a miracle, from what I hear. I wonder what that could mean?" Keid remarked.

This got the older man to stop short and whirl around in front of him to get in his face.

"He is not a tool for you to use in furthering your agenda. We will give him care and shelter until he is well enough to leave, and that will be the end of it."

"For someone to suffer such a terrible beating, then crawl over a mile through dense forest, and finally endure a horrible fever is no small thing. I have no desire to use anyone, yet I cannot help but think that God is with this young man and he was brought to us for a reason," Keid argued.

The abbot glared at him, his brown eyes burning into his own, and held up a finger to punctuate his next point.

"Stay away from him," he demanded before walking away. This time Keid let him go, but that didn't mean he was going to drop the issue.

Chapter Three

Ripples In The Pond

On her way out of the monastery's main building after tending to Raldus, Abbot Jerald stopped Ariela after she entered the front room into the space under the indoor balcony the senior monks often used for non-worship related meetings with the order. The shadows cast by the wooden columns danced around them from the enormous blaze in the main fireplace, an effect which also turned him into a hulking shadow standing before her.

"How is he?"

"He is healing well and his strength begins to return, Abbot," she answered, respectfully keeping her eyes toward the floor.

"How are you doing?" he asked next, causing her heart to skip a beat.

"I'm fine," she gasped, unsure of how else to answer.

"You've taken good care of him, and still managed to see to all your other chores. You must be exhausted."

"I only do what needs to be done," she insisted as she shifted her weight from one foot to the other.

"No, you do much more, and for that you have my thanks," he told her, then walked away to leave her staring after him with her mouth slightly agape.

What had she done to deserve that?

"There is no reason for you to speak to him!" Jerald declared, having long tired of the conversation. He remained seated behind his desk while the other monk stood in front with hands placed squarely upon it, his brown eyes burning with passion.

"There's also no reason not to!" Keid responded in a similar, but quieter, tone. This monk, twenty years his junior, thought he knew better about the spiritual needs of their people than the head of their order who had looked after them for decades.

"He is dangerous, and he will be gone once he has regained his strength."

"You assume that everyone outside our walls is dangerous! Our faith is not meant to be hidden away. Our Lord wants all people to know him, and here is a chance to spread his word."

"These people already rejected him. They tried to kill us once for speaking against their gods, and I'm not about to give them reason to try again!"

"That was generations ago, before even you were born! We can't hide forever!"

"Those we have seen since then haven't given us any reason to trust them now. My answer is final, and you will stay away from the outsider."

The younger monk dropped his chin to chest and sighed, then straightened up and looked at the abbot with a sense of forced patience.

"He has been here for five days. It made sense to maintain space while his fever raged, but he's been lucid for nearly two days now. It might take him many months to heal. Is he to be alone that whole time?"

"I will not discuss this any further," Jerald concluded, then stared at his junior until he left with a swirl of his robes.

The small group of monks standing together in a dark corner of the main building, all of them Keid's age or younger, eagerly huddled around him when he approached. Although they were all of similar height, he couldn't help but feel small among them given his lean frame, yet the fire in his soul more than made up for any lack of size.

"His mind is set and he's stubborn as ever," he revealed with a sigh.

"Why is he so determined to keep us from speaking to the stranger?"

"All we want to do is share our faith with him. That is something an abbot should want."

"He knows that if we were to have any success, it would make everyone reconsider our isolation," Keid explained.

"We can't live this way forever!"

"How can he not want to help people? So many out there we can help, who die without ever being given the choice of eternal life."

"It isn't that he doesn't want to help people. The fact he has taken the stranger in at all is proof of that, but he fears for all of us here. He thinks if the Naerans find out we are here teaching that their gods are false, they will come and destroy us," Keid told them.

"Why would they do that?" the youngest of their group asked, and all the others glared at him with a mixture of pity and humor.

"Study the founding of the monastery and you will find your answer."

"I know the story!"

"Evidently you do not, or you would not ask such a question."

The young man started to respond, but was interrupted by one of the others.

"What are we going to do about the stranger?"

"We will find a way to speak with him. There is much we can teach him, and much we can learn. Jerald will block us, but there are ways.

Pray that God will show them to us and be ready to act when the time comes," Keid concluded before walking away.

"The stranger is your responsibility. He is to be watched at all times, and none of Keid's followers are to be assigned to this duty," Jerald laid out for Ammit, the fifty-seven-year-old bald monk standing before his desk with hands in his sleeves.

"Would it really hurt to let them talk to this man?"

"We don't know what could happen. All that is certain is that this is a man of violence and we must protect our people from him, both their bodies and minds."

"I understand, and I will see to it," Ammit responded as he bowed slightly, then he shuffled away.

Sighing, Jerald stood, his creaking joints reminding him once again of his age, then stood by the stained glass window behind his desk, a simple image of a red circle with blue around and inside, and looked out over all of Our Sacred Refuge. From here he could see the dining hall for the monastery, but the chapel near its northwest corner was just out of his sight. Below the hill, he could see the homes of the farmers and the tiny shapes of the men themselves hard at work in the fields.

Their parents and grandparents suffered much before being forced into this dark forest. Then they found this hill with a bit of open space around it, an island in a sea of trees with nearby water sources, and built a place of safety for themselves and their children with much toil. Here the monks could pray and study while the townspeople worked the land, all of them looking to the needs of the other and doing so in peace.

He would not allow those inside or outside to shatter that peace.

Chapter Four
Sanctuary

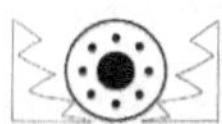

"I've been confined to this room for over a week and I want to see this place," Raldus demanded in a firm tone, without raising his voice.

"Your wounds are many and deep. If you move too much, you will slow your healing and cause more harm," the girl, whose name he'd learned was Ariela fret Imri, patiently explained. She had just finished replacing his bandages and now stood between him and the door, undeterred by his size as she blocked his attempts to leave. His current guard stood inside the door itself trying to look stern, but failing thanks to his lean frame dwarfed in gray robes.

"I'm rotting away in here!"

"You will heal in time, but only if you allow it," Ariela insisted, then she turned to the monk and told him that their guest must remain in the room.

After she left, Raldus stared at the man blocking his way. It would not be difficult to remove him as an obstacle, no matter his own condition, but he had no desire to hurt any of these people. They had shown him nothing but kindness, other than denying him the freedom to move around. Their motivations remained unclear, but he would not repay them with violence without cause.

So he settled on giving the monk a polite nod before sitting at the small table to eat his breakfast.

The shutters swung open to reveal a night sky sparkling with stars but no moon that Raldus could see. He glanced to both sides to confirm no one was present, then over his shoulder at his door which remained closed with the candlelight filtering through remaining undisturbed.

His left arm remained bandaged to his chest, forcing him to rely solely on his right arm to pull himself up into the window. As he did so, the broken wrist sent shooting pain up his arm and into his neck. He grit his teeth, then pulled himself up, swung his legs over, and jumped to the ground a few feet below where he landed in a crouch. His legs almost gave out from the impact, and a fresh wave of pain surged through his entire being, but his training and strong muscles kept him steady.

When he was sure that no one had noticed him, he slowly stood up and took stock of his surroundings. A stone wall over ten feet high stood a few yards in front of him, and even he had to admit that he couldn't climb that one-handed.

He had landed on a stone walkway which went a few yards to his right before turning a corner, while a few feet to his left it became a set of stairs going down. This had to lead somewhere. Not wanting to risk someone being around the corner, he chose to go down the stairs while staying as close to the building as possible, ready to hide in its shadow at the slightest sound.

There turned out to be many steps, so it took him a few minutes to traverse them, but he reached the bottom without incident to find himself in a garden, the sweet aroma of the spring flowers still filling the air. Neatly manicured grass covered the ground, vines crept up the building foundation to his left, and below them was a well-kept bed of flowers of multiple varieties, their colors hidden behind their closed petals. Many paces in front of him, he could just make out a stone fence behind yet more flowers.

Was this place an endless maze of dead ends?

He kept looking from his position at the bottom of the stairs, and upon turning to his right, spotted a thin monk standing beside a small pool and staring into it. Raldus moved to go back up the stairs before the man noticed his presence, but the sudden movement caused his injured shoulder to pop loudly, startling the monk who then fixed him with a wide-eyed look.

"Well, I didn't expect to see you here. I suppose you are in the process of escaping our evil clutches?" the monk teased, his expression morphing from surprise to amusement. This was one Raldus hadn't seen before, and his affable manner contrasted with the others, which gave him pause.

"I don't like sitting still, but I don't think you're evil," he responded, eliciting a small chuckle from the man.

"That's good. I wouldn't mind having some company. Will you walk with me?"

Confused, Raldus just nodded in the affirmative and warily walked up to the monk, whose smile grew at the sight of his guardedness.

"It is a late hour to find oneself in a garden, is it not?" the monk commented as they began their stroll.

"Who takes care of all this?" Raldus asked as he looked around, studying his environment and seeing not a single blade of grass out of place.

"We do."

"Priests?"

His answer came in the form of a casual nod as the monk watched him with a studious yet mellow expression.

He had never known of religious leaders being involved in physical labor, except for those who trained in combat for their devotion to

Malius, the god of heroes. However, he decided not to share this realization with his conversation partner.

"My name is Keid fodi Mekail, and I am faced with a particularly vexing problem. I thought it might help to come here to pray and seek inspiration. God is easily felt in such places, wouldn't you agree?" the monk changed the subject.

"I don't think about it much."

"How do you practice your belief?"

"I don't believe in much of anything beyond what I can do for myself."

"Interesting," Keid remarked.

They were both silent for a moment as they continued to walk, Keid leading and keeping the pace slow in clear deference to his guest, a fact which roused both annoyance and gratitude within the warrior. Crickets chirped in the pleasant night while frogs croaked around an unseen body of water nearby, heralds of the warming weather. As he listened and breathed deep of the fresh air, Raldus found himself appreciative to be outside, but he never let down his guard nor ceased his study of the layout.

"It truly is a beautiful garden. The younger ones do most of the work while the older among us do little more than sit around and talk. Still, I can't help but recognize all the work that goes into it. There are many beautiful things in this world, are there not?"

This time, Raldus didn't react at all, given that he didn't care all that much. The skill and effort he did appreciate, but the looks of things mattered little compared to their usefulness.

"Yes, there is much beauty to be had, works far beyond the ability of men to create. How do you suppose they came to be?" Keid pressed.

"Does it matter?"

"Nothing could be more important," Keid responded, but as they turned away from the wall to retrace their steps, they saw three other monks approaching them, preventing him from saying anything further. The one in the middle being Raldus' current keeper.

"You need to go back," the guard declared as the other two took up positions on either side of the warrior who didn't miss the angry looks cast at Keid.

"I'll take my leave of you now. It was a pleasure to speak with you," Keid told him, then walked off.

Raldus watched him go, wondering as to his nature and motivations, then nodded to the guards to indicate he would cooperate. The possible reasons for his confinement had grown more interesting, but they still hadn't shown any real hostility and he was tired anyway, plus the trek back to his room would reveal more of this place to him.

They followed the same path and entered the building through a door near to his window, the darkness having concealed it when he first passed that way. Inside was a set of stairs next to a hallway off which were connecting passages, but they took the steps to the next level and turned back toward his room.

Although it wasn't much, what he saw provided him with a better understanding of the layout of this place, and that was enough for now.

Upon entering the now candlelit room, he discovered Ariela already waiting for him. Two of the monks left, but the guard remained in the room as she double-checked the bandages.

Dark circles under her eyes revealed a deep fatigue, and when he peered into those hazel circles, he realized they weren't quite in focus and he understood that she had been roused from sleep to come check on him. He felt a lump forming in his throat and glanced away to hide the twinge of remorse threatening to make him feel guilty for having done nothing wrong.

She finished a few minutes later, said he was fine, and left without another word or a single complaint.

The monk shot him a pointed glare, then blew out the candle and closed the door on his way out, leaving Raldus to consider the motivations of his caretaker in the dark.

It made little sense for her to put so much effort into helping him out of obligation alone, but what else could there be? The warrior code on which he was raised required him to stand in harm's way for strangers, but he'd met no one who would sacrifice so much of their time, effort, and resources to restore the health of someone they'd never met.

What drove these people, and what would they ultimately demand of him in return?

Chapter Five

The Board Is Set

The rocks under Tallio's hand lent solidity to the consuming darkness threatening to collapse in on him, smothering him and his name for all eternity. He cleared his throat and licked his lips, but his mouth remained dry and there was no relief for his chapped lips.

Death stalked him in this place, and awaited him behind. Nowhere for him to go but deeper into these infernal rocks.

Maybe he was already dead, his spirit doomed to wander this endless maze which offered no relief for the pain tearing at his gut.

Curse the republic and their soldiers! They'd chased him from every town and city, no matter how strong a gang he gathered for himself. This forced him to travel to that cursed desert over the mountains in search of fortune, but at least he found freedom in that lawless land.

When he'd gathered enough strong men, whose loyalty was without question, he had returned home to take the life which was rightfully his. He was living free in paradise, far from the dust and heat, and not laboring every second of every day for no reward other than survival.

Then the soldiers came.

They always came.

Once again, they destroyed everything he'd gathered for himself. His men were dead and he would be too if he hadn't fled into a crevice in the cliffside. Then those curs made camp right outside, laughing as they dared him to come retrieve his things, and he was left with no choice but to go deeper with the hope of finding a way out.

That was two days ago, and he'd seen nothing but bare stone since. During the day, light shone down from high above, so he wasn't underground even though he might as well be with no way to climb these sheer rock walls.

Why couldn't they just leave him alone?

His legs suddenly buckled and he fell forward. He attempted to catch himself with his outstretched left arm, only for it to collapse under his weight, resulting in his head smashing against the bare ground. The metallic scent of blood mingled with that of dust and dirt as he lay sprawled out, his quickened breath from the surprise now slowing.

The cool stone actually felt good, he admitted to himself as sleep crept in. Perhaps he should rest for a bit. He'd been walking so long, driven on by sheer stubbornness. Surely there wasn't anything ahead that couldn't wait a few minutes.

No!

The word tore through his mind to drive away the weakness, and he clenched his jaw and fists to take hold of that feeling. His life would not end like this.

First getting one hand under him, then the other, he pushed himself up onto his knees, then he reached out until he could grab the rock wall and use it to pull himself the rest of the way up.

He took a deep breath, then resumed moving forward with feet shuffling along the ground with right hand on the wall while his left stretched forward in search mode.

A blast of fresh air struck him, its sweet scent refreshing his body and soul as he breathed deep, spurring him into a marginally faster pace.

When he finally emerged into the open, his arms dropped to his sides as he closed his eyes and breathed deep, a smile forming on his face.

He'd beaten them again! He was going to live!

Then he opened his eyes, and his heart froze in his chest as the shadowy form of a man at least a hundred-feet tall filled his vision, his glowing red eyes staring right at him. Beyond it a crimson glow illuminated dozens of spires reaching toward the sky, the sight driving him to his knees as he clasped his hands to beg the gods' forgiveness.

"Agh!" he grunted as he shot up in bed, covered in a cold sweat.

His eyes darted in all directions as he gasped for air, reality slowly setting in as the canvas tent rustled in a gentle breeze. When his breathing steadied, he threw aside the thin blanket and swung his feet out of the sturdy bed, the grass tickling his feet as he stomped over to the table next to the center pole.

He snatched up the clay pitcher, poured the brown ale into a bronze goblet, and downed the bitter drink in a single gulp.

With his courage restored, he strode over to the entrance and pushed aside a flap to stand there staring into the east. The dream and the memory which spawned it melded together to become impossible to tell one from the other.

There could be no doubt that Republic soldiers had killed his last gang and driven him into the unexplored mountains marking the southeastern border, but what had come after that was another matter. He had told nobody of the people he'd met deep in that waste of rock and stone, those who had built the colossus in his dream, and he often wondered if it had ever been anything *but* a dream.

Yet it couldn't be denied that he wouldn't be here now if it weren't for them, their resources keeping him one step ahead of the soldiers and even the mercenaries the senate had hired to hunt him down.

He let out a single grunt, then let the tent flap fall into place and went back to bed. Dream or not, he was well on his way to gaining the power and riches he'd always desired and the past no longer mattered.

"You are not leaving this family to run around like a childish fool!" Farela screamed at her husband as he threw open the door to their house, not caring if the neighbors heard her at this point.

"Don't tell me what to do, woman!" Decius shouted back as he whirled around to face her, leaving the door to hang open as he balled his hands into fists at his sides. The baby started crying in the corner, her wails summoning her two older sisters over to the crib to comfort her.

"Someone has to stop you from getting yourself killed and us thrown into the street!" Farela stood up to him, earning herself a backhand to the face which sent her sprawling against the oak table behind her.

Now the baby was screaming at the top of her lungs, mingling with her sisters' sobs as they gave up trying to calm her in favor of huddling together for protection.

"I will waste no more of my life in this hovel with a bunch of girls. This man Tallio has power and gets more treasure every day. I'm going to get my piece while I can," Decius snarled as he towered over her.

Silent tears rolled down her face as she held the rapidly swelling cheek with her right hand, but she refused to make a sound in her distress or let him leave guilt-free.

"What kind of man leaves his wife and daughters destitute while he chases after riches?" she accused, her voice not much louder than a whisper.

A slammed door was her only answer, and she slumped to the dirt floor, holding both hands over her face as the tears flowed free.

"We are unstoppable!" Tallio shouted as he rode past the short tents and up to the unlit campfire ring on a brown stallion, reveling in the cheers of his men. He took a long drink of wine from the gourd in his right hand while the others dismounted and their comrades rushed forward to grab the bags filled with jewels and gold.

The bandit leader guffawed at the sight of his men's ecstasy, but his laughter cut short when he spotted a man in dark armor and holding a tall staff standing on a small hill behind the camp. Grunting, he tossed the gourd aside, swung off his horse, and stomped up to the intruder.

The man's skin was the color of bronze, his hair dark and short, and the dark blue metal armor covering his entire body save the head had raised ridges running horizontally, which served no other purpose than style. The staff rested on the ground and appeared to be made of gold. Intricate designs adorned the shaft, and a diamond-shaped glass piece held in place by gold tendrils sat at the top.

The dream from the other night flashed in his mind as he walked, now feeling like a premonition out of which this man had stepped. He briefly wondered if these people had the power to announce their coming this way, but banished the thought as absurd.

"What are you doing here? I was told I'm in charge," Tallio challenged, looking up into the interloper's clear blue eyes. He'd never met this man, but did know his master, the identity of which was revealed by the purplish ring around the collar of his armor and stripe on each shoulder.

"You are in charge. My people are ready to enact the next phase of the plan. I am here to coordinate our efforts."

"I will not have any of you getting in my way. I don't care what you've done for me."

"We have no desire to interfere. My only purpose is to observe and communicate to the city what transpires."

"Everything here is mine. They agreed."

"That agreement does not preclude the presence of an observer," the stranger assured him. Upon seeing Tallio's expression, he added, "We didn't say we couldn't watch."

"So you're not going to do anything?"

“Keep doing what you are doing, and you won’t even notice I’m here.”

The bandit studied the observer. Even after spending time in their city, these people remained a mystery to him, but they had kept every promise, so there was no reason for him not to believe this agent of theirs.

“What is your name?” Tallio questioned.

“You do not need to know my name, only whom I serve,” the stranger replied, his tone low with an implied threat.

Tallio’s hand raised without him realizing, but he lowered it once he did notice and swallowed to push down the pride rising within him.

“So be it,” he growled before turning and walking away. He spotted one of his men watching wide-eyed, so upon reaching him, he grabbed him by the front of the tunic and shoved him into the dirt.

Feeling a little better now, he smiled and returned to the party, not caring to notice as the observer turned the other way and headed off on his own toward the sunset.

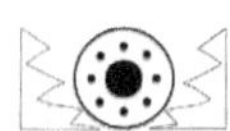

“No!” Raldus shouted as he shot up in bed covered in sticky sweat, which had soaked into his bandages. His eyes probed the darkness as he leaned over and searched the floor for a sword with his right hand.

Then the images faded, his breathing slowed, and he returned to sitting straight up as he remembered where he was. Pain shot through his entire body without the excitement to numb it, and he lowered himself back down.

“I don’t lose. I never lose,” he whispered, attempting to drive the images, the memories, from his mind.

Yet when he closed his eyes, all he could see was the laughing face of that bandit as his men beat Raldus, one unrelenting blow after another.

Chapter Six

Matters of Faith

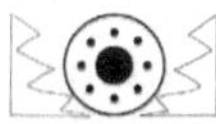

After nearly three weeks of being cooped up, Raldus started exercising as much as he could in his small room, a process which improved considerably when Ariela freed his left arm from his chest a week later. The bandages remained to prevent him from bending it at the elbow or wrist, but at least he could move it around now and work the shoulder along with the other arm.

Shortly thereafter, the monks had deigned to allow him to move around the monastery, but always with an escort and never to the town. It was now over a month since he'd arrived, and for lack of anything better to do, he had been observing the monks and their rituals, discovering their beliefs to be unlike anything he'd ever seen before.

For starters, they emphasized that their acts of service were motivated solely by a desire to honor their god and not by a need to earn his favor. They even said that no one could earn his favor, but he still gave it to all people merely for accepting his existence and authority.

Then there was the story about him coming in the form of a mortal man and allowing himself to be killed for their sake. That didn't make any sense to him, but they weren't offering to explain it and he wasn't stooping to asking them questions.

When he was first allowed to wander, Ariela had come around at least twice a day to check on him, then only once a day, and now he only saw her three or four times a week. Each time she cleaned wounds, replaced bandages, and reminded him to be careful no matter how fast he was healing, but never spoke about anything else.

Today he was walking the perimeter of the courtyard, not running or jogging as he would have liked, but still going fast enough to wear out his escort and cause him to wait in the center instead. When he saw her coming, he went straight to his room with her following and sat on the edge of the bed after removing his tunic.

"What do you believe in?" he asked after she'd set to work.

"What do you mean?" she questioned, a brief pause in her work revealing her surprise.

"Do you and the others in the town follow the same god as the monks?" he clarified. His questions had drawn the attention of his guard, who paid close attention but did not interfere.

"Yes," she answered while avoiding his gaze.

"Why?"

"What do you mean?"

"Do you decide this for yourselves or do they require it of you?" he explained while keeping an eye on the guard, who continued to watch and listen without intervening.

"They teach us, but we choose our own way."

"Why are you helping me?"

"Rosjen tells us to help all who are in need."

"Even those who don't serve him?"

This question finally caused her to meet his gaze in surprise.

"His love and mercy is freely offered to all people," the monk answered for her, and it was Raldus' turn to be surprised, although his training kept him from showing it as he gave the man a few years his senior a passive look. Until now, none of the monks had addressed him directly about their beliefs and he'd always sensed an underlying fear anytime he watched them.

"You are healing well, but still at risk of causing new harm. Remember to get plenty of rest," Ariela spoke up before Raldus could say anything else, then hurriedly gathered her things and left the room. The monk gave him a look he couldn't decipher, then stepped outside without closing the door.

"Why are you here?" Jerald demanded to know of the warrior whom he'd found performing stretches beside the pool in the monk's garden.

"You brought me here," Raldus responded after pausing his routine and giving the abbot a confused look.

"You misunderstand me. Why are you still here? A warrior such as yourself is surely capable of walking to the nearest town by now."

"If it was necessary, but it isn't. How can anyone believe in only one god?"

The quick switch in topic caught Jerald off-guard. When he couldn't think of a response, he spun around and stormed off.

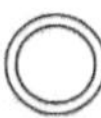

"I thought that you don't contemplate such things?" Keid questioned as he stepped out from under the tree from where he had observed the confrontation.

"Most people choose a single god to serve, but they still believe in the others and usually honor them in some way," Raldus deflected.

"What makes any of these beings worthy of service?"

"They are gods."

"What makes them gods?"

"They have great power."

"Have you ever witnessed that power? Has anyone?"

"I don't know."

"What have they ever done for us mere mortals?"

"They protect us from evil."

"But only as long as you please them?"

"I suppose," Raldus admitted. Keid's smile radiated warmth as he stepped up to the young man to make his next point.

"Our god came to save us from ourselves and offers this as a gift to anyone who chooses to accept it. He didn't make us prove ourselves to him, but instead proved himself to us."

Jerald stood atop the steps leading down to the town, looking out over it but too deep in his own mind to see any of it. A gentle breeze ruffled his clothes and stirred his hair and long beard, instilling a sense of peace and comfort alongside its coolness.

"This is what I have been warning you about," Keid's voice admonished from behind, snapping him back to reality in a most irritating fashion.

"I don't recall requesting your opinion," the elder monk shot back as the troublemaker took up position beside him.

"You never do," Keid joked, but Jerald didn't laugh.

"It doesn't mean anything."

"It means that we aren't prepared to answer questions. We are charged with spreading Rosjen's word to all people. How are we supposed to do that when we can't answer even the simplest of questions about him?"

"The ability to answer a question matters little when one is dodging a stone thrown at his head," Jerald asserted, then he turned and walked away.

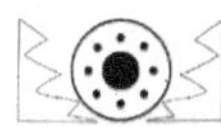

After saying nothing to him for over three days, Jerald suddenly summoned Raldus to meet with him in his office.

The room was modestly adorned, the singular window of red and blue glass the most prominent feature. In front of it was an oak desk with an angled top and matching chairs, one behind and the other in front. As the sunlight filtered through the colored window, it cast a soft and serene light, creating a peaceful ambiance. To the right of the door opposite the window, three candles burned atop a tall stand, illuminating that side of the room with their steady flames.

Upon arriving, the warrior offered no greeting as he stood next to the guest chair and glared at the gray-bearded old man seated behind it. His host sat with his hands on the desktop as he silently regarded Raldus, who prepared himself for a contest of wills, the first round of which would be seeing who spoke first.

"What do you believe?" the abbot finally questioned.

"I've already been through this with one of your monks," Raldus balked.

"Now I want you to tell me."

The warrior let out a long sigh and rolled his eyes toward the ceiling, where they remained as he answered.

"I've never thought that much about it."

"Your people didn't teach you their beliefs?"

This got him to look back at the abbot with a confused expression he couldn't conceal.

"They taught me to fight."

"Is that all? Nothing about how to live? Nothing about how this world came to be or why?"

"I heard plenty of stories, but my instructors mostly focused on the code," Raldus revealed, feeling a bit curious as to where the old man was going with this despite himself.

"The code? Tell me about that."

"The Stoneforge Warrior Code tells us who to fight, when to fight, and when not to."

"Tell it to me."

"Why?"

The abbot said nothing and just kept watching him with the same analytical expression. Sighing again, he decided to go ahead and say the creed, as he was in no mood to recite the whole thing.

Honor Over Vanity
Home Over Wealth
Others Over Self

Strength To Serve
Courage To Stand
Wisdom To Live

Fighter, Not Barbarian
Defender, Not Oppressor
Equal, Not Superior

Forged by stone of earth and
fire of spirit.

They were both silent as Jerald processed the words while stroking his long gray beard with his eyes down.

"And this doesn't come as part of service to a deity?" he clarified.

"No."

"Interesting."

"Why do you care?" Raldus exclaimed, growing tired of being interrogated.

"We have been isolated from your world for a long time. I doubt anything has changed, but through you, I can gain clarity."

"What are you so scared of?"

The abbot looked at him, prompting a twinge of guilt in Raldus when he saw a deep sadness there.

"You can leave now," Jerald declared, then pulled a quill from its holder and began writing on the half-filled parchment in the center of the desk.

The warrior huffed, then spun on one heel and stomped off; any guilt gone thanks to the rude dismissal.

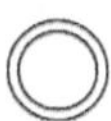

Stepping out into the warm sun after praying in the chapel, Keid spotted their guest in the middle of the plaza, earnestly looking around at every monk in sight. When their gazes met, the young man strolled toward him despite the protestations of Brother Yahud, his current escort.

"Why are you hiding here, and what does it have to do with me?" Raldus demanded to know upon reaching the chapel steps.

"It has nothing to do with you," Yahud insisted, but Raldus ignored him and kept looking at Keid for an answer.

"Our people came to this land from a distant country in the east. Our grandparents attempted to share their faith with your people, but were rebuffed at every turn. Eventually, annoyance turned to violence and they fled into this forest for safety. They found a place to rest and recover, and what was meant to be nothing more than a camp became a town," the monk explained as Yahud kept looking between them and the main building.

"That was a long time ago. Why be scared of me and keep secrets?"

"Abbot Jerald believes that if people learn we are here, they will come and finish the job."

Raldus grew thoughtful at this and looked at the ground while Keid gave a reassuring smile to the young monk watching him, but it did little good to ease his anxiety.

Several seconds passed, then the warrior turned to leave, but stopped to say one last thing over his shoulder.

"If that's the case, wouldn't it have been better for him to let me die?"

"That is not our way, no matter the possible danger."

Chapter Seven

Pieces on a Board

"This is almost too easy," Tallio commented to himself as he looked at the chest full of gold and jewels beside the bed in his tent. Over two hundred men followed him at this point, most of them in five camps spread around the countryside with the rest making up mobile raiding parties. They didn't have a lot of armor available to them, and what they did have rarely matched, but all of them were well-supplied with food and weapons.

He wondered if he should use some of this money to fully outfit his followers, or start hiring mercenaries, but he banished the idea with a shake of his head. Why buy what he could steal, and there were always plenty of fools willing to follow him for whatever scraps he chose to throw their way.

"Boss!" someone shouted over the whinnying of a horse being pulled to an abrupt stop. Tallio slammed down the chest lid, then shoved the tent flap out of his way and marched up to the recent arrival.

"What!" he demanded as the rider, not yet old enough to be called a man, jumped down from his horse.

"The legions are being sent to Esbera! They've started another war! Anyone hunting us has been called back!" the boy explained between gasps.

Every bandit who heard the news cheered and declared their newfound freedom to truly do as they pleased, but Tallio grew quiet and thoughtful.

"What's wrong?" someone asked, but he just sneered at him, then stomped off to the east side of the camp.

There he found the observer standing outside his dark blue silk tent, staring toward the mountains that separated Naeran lands from Esbera.

"What is this about a war?" he demanded to know.

"My people have convinced the Esberan lords to unite against the Naeran Republic and reclaim their stolen land."

"Those fools never work together."

"All people have their price. Some are swayed by money, others by threats, and my people know all means of persuasion. They will do as instructed."

The observer had yet to look away from the mountains as they talked, but now Tallio stepped around to stand inches away, forcing him to look down at him as he made his next statement.

"The deal was that I will rule. I will not share power with those desert rats!" he spit, but his anger turned to confusion when the observer gave him an amused smile.

"They are merely a distraction, a tool to weaken the Naerans and allow you to operate. You are the only one aware of our true nature and intentions. They know nothing. They *are* nothing."

"You aren't helping them like you are me?"

"Only what is required to make them a credible threat. Now that the legions are gone, you will be able to take control of the countryside. Your ranks will swell, and your enemies will be capable of nothing more than cowering in their cities."

"I'm not doing this to take charge of a bunch of farmers," Tallio growled, but the observer's amusement only grew.

"Fear not. All is going according to plan and you will have what you seek soon enough," he assured.

The bandit paused to think. There was something about that smile he didn't like, as if this man knew more than he was saying, but then again, these people pretty much always looked like that.

"Good enough," he finally grunted, then walked away.

"There's nothing here!" Calvis shouted as he kicked over the chest his two sons had tossed down from the wagon, spilling the tunics and belts into the ditch.

"We don't have anything else. Please don't hurt us," the young man on his knees in the road beside the cart pleaded with his clasped hands held up toward Calvis. The traveler's wife sat to his right, choking back sobs as she stared down at the folds of her red cotton dress over her thighs.

"There is always something else," the raid leader observed in a low tone as he turned and looked down at his victims. The man's eyes grew wide as a multitude of scenarios raced through his mind, but the woman continued to avoid Calvis' gaze.

Then Calvis took a slow step toward her, but the man shot to his feet to stand in his way, so he backhanded him across the face to send him stumbling into the side of the cart.

"Vissus!" the woman cried out upon looking up to see her husband holding his face in both hands with blood streaming through his fingers. She rose with hands reaching toward him, but Calvis shoved her and she fell back onto her butt.

"So, you do have some heart after all," Calvis mocked as his eldest son grabbed the traveler by the shoulders and forced him back to his knees. Meanwhile, the youngest kept staring at the woman from behind and to her right, and Calvis glanced at him before looking back at his victims with a wicked smile.

“Since you have some fight in you, you will come join us. Your wife can stay in the camp cooking and mending, and if you don’t do as you’re told, I’ll kill you and give her to my boy here.”

The man Vissus looked at the teenager who wet his lips in anticipation, then down at his wife who was now staring at Calvis with mouth agape and tears streaming down her face, and lastly back up at Calvis who awaited his reply with a mocking grin.

Finally, Vissus looked down at the ground and nodded his assent, the hands still holding his face moving up and down with the action.

“Good. You may yet prove to have some value after all. Back to camp!” Calvis concluded. His sons hauled the couple to their feet, after which the wife attempted to pull Vissus’ hands away to tend to his injury, but he shrugged her off. Then the bandits pushed them forward as Calvis led the way into the woods.

Chapter Eight

Matters of Honor

"It is good to see you, Uncle, but it is not yet time for our noonday meal," Ariela greeted the gray-robed monk as she ushered him across the threshold of her home.

"There is much I wish to discuss," Nurin replied as he sat in the kitchen and let out a long sigh.

"Father and Tobias will not return for some time," she told him as she returned to preparing the meal.

"It is you to whom I wish to speak," he revealed.

"What do you need of me?"

"The outsider seems to be doing well under your care."

"His wounds are healing and his strength returns."

"How has he treated you?"

"He tolerates me."

"Does he ever speak of himself or his life?"

"No. He only speaks to answer my questions on his recovery. One time he asked some questions about us, but that's all."

Her uncle grew silent for a moment as if pondering how, or if, he would ask his next question. She did not press him and simply continued with the cooking, even though she couldn't help but wonder why he was so interested in Raldus.

"Would you be willing to speak to him about our faith and teach him our doctrines?" Nurin finally proposed, almost causing her to drop a bowl in surprise.

"It is not my place," she responded after steadying herself.

"The abbot is preventing us from doing so. Keid has managed to say a few things to him, but that is all."

"Abbot Jerald is a wise man," Ariela said evasively, knowing full well the conflict between the abbot and Keid's group, of which her uncle was a member.

"No man is without fault, Ariela. You know that," Nurin chastised.

"It is not my place to be involved with such things," she repeated.

"You are his caretaker, and his spiritual health is every bit as important as that of his flesh."

She did not respond. The meal was almost ready and the others would be here soon.

The monk sighed, then stood up and turned to leave, but not before saying one last thing.

"Please think about it. There are many outside our walls who are lost, and this is a chance to do something about it."

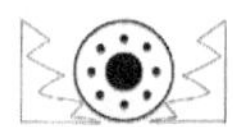

His afternoon walk took Raldus to the stairs leading from the monastery buildings to the town below the hill. As he approached, Ariela and another woman were stepping off carrying baskets full of fresh linens. The girl noticed him first and they exchanged a brief glance, but when the older woman spotted him, she gasped and ran off as fast as she could with the basket tucked under one arm. Ariela looked between her and the warrior twice in surprise, then hurried after her companion.

"That woman is frightened of me, but I have caused no harm," Raldus remarked to his escort.

“Many years ago, when she was but a maiden, another soldier like you found his way here. He was badly in need of food, water, and shelter, so we took him in and cared for him. Once he was well, he did not leave, nor did he work. One day he found that girl alone and forced himself upon her.”

The warrior’s fists clenched as heat rushed through his body, but he kept a calm demeanor as he asked the monk what happened to the soldier without bothering to correct him on the difference between his order and the army.

“The men in the town nearly killed him when they found out, but a monk convinced them to bring him before the abbot, who chose to banish him.”

“He did not live long after that,” Raldus declared, his tone free from any doubt. The monk looked him full in the face with his eyes wide and mouth agape in shock.

“How do you know?”

“Animals like that never do.”

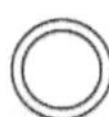

“Those were his exact words?” Keid inquired of the other monk walking with him along the vine-covered stone brick wall separating them from the rest of the world. They had come here for a measure of privacy, but the shade from the ten-foot high wall was a welcome bonus as the day grew warmer.

This young man was one of those assigned to watch the outsider, and he had just finished relating an interaction from the previous afternoon. His response to the question of his elder was a simple nod.

“What of his manner? Could you discern anything about what he was feeling?”

“Tense. It seemed the story had angered him.”

"This surprises you?"

"Yes," the junior replied, trailing off as if he wasn't sure about saying more.

"You can speak your mind."

The two continued in silence for a time, long enough for Keid to fear he would not continue, but then he finally spoke up again.

"I thought that those outside our walls are like that soldier in the story, opposite to us in every way. The entire time I've been watching this one, I have feared he would strike me down at any moment. Now I find myself believing I can trust him."

"The people outside are just as diverse in personality as those within. Their beliefs and personal honor tend to be similarly diverse. Not all can be judged by the actions of one man," Keid explained.

"What of those who drove our ancestors into hiding?"

"That was still only one group, possibly a mob where many were caught up regardless of their personal thoughts and feelings."

"I don't know what to think now."

"Such is the beginning of wisdom," Keid comforted as he wrapped an arm around his companion's shoulders. The younger man nodded in response, his eyes seeing little due to all he had to ponder.

He wasn't the only one. After they separated and returned to their duties, Keid found himself sitting in the chapel's worship hall, staring at the large wooden circle nailed to the wall behind the stage.

The revelation that the warrior took offense at the vile actions of that man so many years ago had surprised him as well, a fact he'd hidden from his junior during their conversation. It would seem that he was just as guilty of deeming everyone outside their walls to be violent, uneducated beasts, no matter how much he advocated the need to end their isolation.

This did not sit right with him. He had been so consumed with battling Jerald's stubbornness that he had failed to see his own mistake.

What kind of man did that make him?

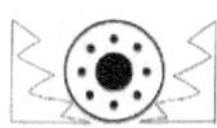

As purpose once again took hold of Raldus' heart, it overshadowed any pain caused by his remaining injuries. For two days he had conducted his exercises where he could see across the town, and his walks grew in length and scope and soon he knew all the paths.

He'd already walked twice as far as usual this afternoon, at twice his normal pace, until his escort was huffing along behind him, looking ready to drop at any moment. He went around the main building towards the monk's garden, but after turning the corner, he darted through a side door, then held it most of the way closed and looked out through the gap.

The monk appeared a few seconds later and stopped short when he didn't see his charge. He looked all around him in near panic, then ran down the stairs.

When he was gone, Raldus stepped back outside and made his way around the back of the building, not taking the stairs but instead walking along the edge between the building and the drop above the garden.

On the other side, he carefully descended the hill to come out next to a large, uneven oval pool of water where he'd seen the women go to wash clothes. He stayed back long enough to identify his target, then swiftly walked up behind her where she stood ankle deep in the water and stopped beside her basket on the bank. Her companion on the right gasped upon seeing him, and they all stopped their work to stare as the older one before him spun around before stumbling backward as if to flee, barely catching herself before falling from the sudden movement.

"Do not be afraid," he said as he held his hands up at chest height, palms out, calming her enough to stop before she wandered into deeper water. He stayed back, out of reach, but close enough to block her escape.

"What do you want?" she gasped. The other women stayed back, making no move to interfere or run.

"I was told what happened to you and I felt it important to tell you that you have no reason to fear me. It is my purpose in life to protect people and to rid the world of brutes such as the one who harmed you."

"You're a soldier, just like he was," she stammered. At this point, one of the others came up to her and wrapped her shoulders in a hug. He recognized the newcomer as Ariela, but did not acknowledge her.

"No, I am a warrior sworn to a code, not a government. That code guides me in all that I do and holds no room for such evil."

Her fear faded somewhat to become mixed with confusion as she looked up at him with wide eyes. Having said what was on his heart, Raldus nodded and walked away without another word.

He used the stairs to go back up the hill, then headed to the monk's garden to find his escort whom he hoped hadn't fainted in the interim.

"How dare you!" Jerald shouted as he advanced on Raldus, who was currently stretching in the center of the monastery plaza.

Before the warrior had a chance to respond, Keid rushed up from Jerald's right to stand to the side between him and their guest. The abbot glared at him, but the man only looked back with a blank expression.

"I have done nothing wrong," Raldus insisted.

"You terrorized that woman!"

"I did no such thing."

The abbot's jaw clenched so tight it felt his teeth would shatter. Keid kept watching with the same blank look, but Raldus stood there calmly, while the monk who had replaced his exhausted escort from an hour earlier looked ready to bolt.

"There is no more reason for you to remain here. Leave this place," Jerald finally declared. The warrior's only response at first was to watch him with that infuriatingly passive gaze, but then he shrugged and started to walk away, but Keid stopped him.

"This isn't right, and you know it," he directed at Jerald, who proceeded to fix his rage-filled gaze upon his rival.

"He is dangerous."

"The story I heard says that he kept his distance while speaking, then left in peace. He hasn't done anything to anyone."

"He tricked his escort so he could get away and threaten the women!"

"He could have attacked and even killed the monk to get away, but didn't. Again, from what I hear, he only talked to them and was careful to not be threatening."

"This only proves that he can't be trusted!"

"On the contrary, it proves that he can. Even unsupervised, he caused no harm and willingly returned to his escort once he had accomplished his task."

By now, the argument had attracted the attention of several other monks, and Jerald looked around to see all of them listening intently. Most appeared indecisive, which might be a problem.

"If anything, he has shown that he doesn't even require an escort," Keid added. Jerald looked back at him, then over to Raldus who still showed no emotion, and lastly surveyed the crowd again before settling his gaze on the outsider.

"Remain if you wish. You will no longer be watched," he consented, then walked off, ignoring the whispers of the monks.

The nearly full moon lit Ariela's way as she climbed some boxes to the top of the northern wall, then swung her legs over before lightly dropping to the other side, the fall proving to be shorter than she remembered. She darted into the trees, energized by the myriad of feelings she'd suppressed all afternoon, the release now banishing all fatigue from her mind and limbs as she made her way through the woods.

It wasn't long before she emerged into the open again next to a pond, and she sat on a flat rock to peer into the murky water with the light of the moon and stars shining upon its surface. Frogs croaked, a number of small animals rustled among the trees, and a wolf howled in the distance, but she felt no danger as she sat breathing in the smells of mud and fish while listening to the water lapping at the bank.

When the outsider had arrived, she couldn't believe he still drew breath after suffering so much and fully expected he wouldn't live much longer, but knew that tending to him was still the right thing to do. She had cleaned and bandaged his wounds, then stayed at his side to soothe him as much as possible as he thrashed and shouted from the fever, thinking only of providing some manner of comfort for him at the end.

Yet, he came through the fever and began to heal. She continued as his caretaker, happy to help in any way possible, but it was only a job to be done, one of many. The world from whence he came meant nothing, and if he lived, he would return to it and she would continue in hers as if he had never been, but now something had changed.

When she first saw him standing over Zohara at the pool, every word Jerald had ever spoke regarding the dangers of the outside world flooded her mind and she couldn't decide between running for help or hiding her face from the horror that was surely coming next. She found all she could do was watch, but as she did, a strange sense of calm came over her and she became intent on sharing that calm with her frightened friend.

When Raldus spoke, he was calm but passionate. He had been careful not to reveal his thoughts or feelings this entire time, but now she could see that his proclamation of desiring to protect people and rid the world of evil was honest and heartfelt, revealing a deep compassion within him. Hearing those words and seeing how much Zohara's fear bothered him revealed a depth to him Ariela had only ever seen in the monks, sparking an intense curiosity about him and his world.

Even though she continued insisting he needed more time to heal, she knew he was strong enough to leave if he desired, and she'd begun to wonder why he hadn't. Was he merely waiting until he was fully healed? What other reason could there be?

When he did leave, what would he be taking with him? What was the world like beyond the walls?

She had been more curious as a child, a curiosity which had driven her to sneak over the wall as often as she could get away with it and explore the surrounding woods, but never straying too far. In doing so, she'd found this place, a perfect spot to be alone and think. When Mother died, she'd set aside such pursuits to take care of her father and baby brother.

She hadn't indulged her curious nature for a long time, but now she realized it had always been there and these events had stoked it into becoming more powerful than ever.

What else was out there for her to find and learn?

Chapter Nine

Matters of the Heart

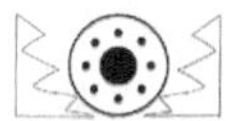

"That's good," Raldus said as he flexed his right wrist and arm, now liberated from its bandages. Greenish bruises still covered the pale skin, but he felt little pain and Ariela told him it was now safe to move freely.

"What does that symbol represent?" she asked with a glance at his forearm while rolling up the used linen. He turned the arm and studied the bold black-ink tattoo of a symbol about which he had given little thought even before the bandage covered it.

"It is the crest of the Stoneforge Warriors and represents both the order and town, but only warriors receive the tattoo upon completing their training," he explained without looking up.

Now he moved it into the light to give her a clearer view and pointed at each piece to explain the symbols themselves.

"These jagged lines on each side represent the ravine that leads to the town, and the shield shows us to be warriors serving our home."

"What is your home like?" she questioned as she moved on to check his left arm.

"Sheer cliffs surround the town on all sides, and it is difficult to reach except through the ravine. It is a safe place, but little grows there, so the warriors hire themselves out to earn the money to buy what we need."

“You said there are other warriors who serve different masters. Is there really enough work for all of you?”

“There are no other warriors in this land,” Raldus responded, confused.

“What about the one who attacked Zohara, the woman you spoke to at the pool?”

“That was a soldier, not a warrior.”

“What’s the difference?”

“It’s not like you to ask so many questions,” he observed, causing her to blush.

“It was strange what you said to Zohara,” she admitted as she finished removing the bandage from his arm. She then asked him to move it around and tell her if he felt any pain.

He bent it back and forth and twisted it around, feeling a fair amount of stiffness and hearing a few pops but little pain, which he reported to her and she revealed that bandage was also no longer needed.

“Soldiers are inducted into the army and trained upon reaching adulthood. It is a temporary service after which they return home. Warriors train their entire lives and remain in that profession until their death,” he continued explaining as she tended to his chest injuries.

“Aren’t soldiers protectors of the people?”

“Yes, but there are many tasks they do not have the skills to take on, and many others that are too small for them to bother. Those are the jobs we do.”

She nodded and silently continued with her work.

“Tell me about your family,” he requested after a minute or two.

“My father and younger brother work in the fields while I tend to the home. Mother died when I was six years old, a year after my other brother died when he was only two months old,” she told him.

“You have so much responsibility yet still manage to tend to me.”

“I do what is needed.”

He gently grasped her wrist and looked deep into her hazel eyes when she stopped and looked up.

"Thank you," he said softly, causing her to tear up a little. When he released her, she quickly recovered and returned to her work.

She finished a few minutes later without replacing any bandages, not even the bindings for his broken ribs.

"You are doing well and don't need me checking on you anymore. Continue to get plenty of rest, and you will be fully healed soon," she concluded as she gathered her things, but she hesitated at the door.

"Will we still be permitted to speak?" he questioned. He sensed that there was more she wanted to know about where he came from, and he had to admit that his own curiosity about these people and their beliefs was getting the better of him.

"Yes," she answered quietly, almost shyly.

"I would be glad to answer any more questions you might have."

She indicated her understanding with a quick nod, then darted out the door.

He donned his tunic again, then stood at the window and looked out to the forest beyond the wall to reflect upon his return to that world. It was no longer an immediate need for him since his quarry had no doubt moved on long ago and he would need to track him down again, no matter when he left. There was also no chance that anyone else had, or would, succeed where he failed unless they tasked the entire army on it.

For now, he would stay here to regain his health and train to be stronger than ever. When the time did come for him to leave, he would do so stronger than ever and none would stand in his way.

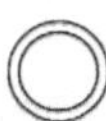

After his bandages were removed, the warrior's first act was to set up a proper training area below the dining hall on the hill and near the town forum a short distance to the north. He hadn't asked for anything, but found some old wood and straw on his own to create a mannequin and archery target. In a move that had surprised everyone, one morning he offered to chop firewood to top off the monastery's supply for no reward other than permission to use the ax afterward. After finishing, he had gone into the forest and cut the wood to make a training sword, a bow, and some arrows.

Approaching this training area, Keid spotted him sitting on the grass, gazing at the straw mannequin as the setting sun lengthened the shadows and cast all in an orange glow.

"When you first awoke, all you could think about was leaving. Now that you are able, you remain," the monk observed with a humorous tone.

"I'm not ready," Raldus replied evenly.

"You are strong enough to travel if you wish."

This time the young man said nothing and kept staring at the target with unseeing eyes. Keid let out a long sigh, then stepped up and took a seat next to the warrior, his gray robes spreading out around him.

"You don't have to face your fears alone," he offered.

"I don't fear anything."

"You know what I mean," Keid challenged. The warrior let out an exasperated sigh in response before standing to dust himself off.

"I suppose you're going to tell me again how your god can solve everything."

"No."

This one word caused the warrior to look down at the still seated monk in surprise, the latter meeting his gaze and looking deep into his green eyes.

"You are not accustomed to fear or doubt, and would never admit it if you felt either of those things now. The only thing I wish to say is that you do not have to face your troubles alone."

"Are you suggesting I join you and stay here?"

"I am suggesting that you consider converting to our faith, but that does not require you to become a monk or stay here."

"Why would I do that?"

"That is not for me to say," Keid answered, then stood while suppressing a groan when his joints protested. He put a hand on the young man's shoulder to guarantee he focused on what he said next.

"Something is keeping you here longer than either you or we expected. Consider what that might be, and allow yourself to follow that line of reasoning."

The monk gave Raldus' shoulder a gentle squeeze, then turned and walked away.

"You sent for me?" Raldus stated with as much respect as he could muster upon entering the abbot's office.

"Take a seat," Jerald ordered without pause to his writing on parchment with quill. The warrior sat down as instructed and prepared himself for another lecture.

Neither spoke as the elderly man continued writing by the light of the sun streaming through the red and blue stained glass window behind him. He'd learned the red circle symbolized the means by which the mortal form of their god was executed centuries ago, a manner called a breaking wheel which was previously unfamiliar to him but he was told is popular in their part of the world. The convict had his wrists bound to the wheel and ankles tied to a stake in the ground, then water dripped into a bucket from a hopper to turn the wheel and stretch him until he suffocated.

A showy business, a style known to be practiced by many foreigners, but the Naerans usually preferred to just get it done and over with.

Shaking his head to clear the images, Raldus looked around the office, which was all too familiar to him by now with its single desk and two chairs, one behind and the other in front. After consenting to allow the warrior to roam the monastery and town as he pleased, the abbot had periodically called him here to preach and ask questions. Yet another way of asserting control.

When he finally finished with what he wanted to write, Jerald lay the quill on the desk above the parchment and looked his guest in the eye.

"What do you think of us?"

"Pardon?" Raldus responded. This was not what he had been expecting.

"What do you think of this place and the people in it?" Jerald rephrased. Raldus studied him, both out of the suspicion this was some sort of trap and to take a moment to think. The old man's face remained unreadable, brown eyes steady and unwavering above his long, gray beard.

"I am grateful for your care and continued hospitality," he answered, choosing his words carefully.

"Is that all?"

This time, Raldus could only nod in response.

"You've learned some things about our faith. What are your thoughts on it?"

Again, Raldus looked into the other man's eyes for some clue as to where he was going with this line of questioning, but still found nothing.

"It's different," he said carefully.

"How so?"

Now his patience was wearing thin, so he decided to just speak plainly.

"I've heard of many gods, yet you believe there is only one and all the others are fakes. Every god I know about demands we serve him, but you claim this one took on human form to serve us and let himself be killed to prove a point."

"Does this offend you?"

"It confuses me."

The abbot stared at him, his expression unchanging, which was really beginning to irritate him.

After a few moments of that, he finally leaned back in his chair as his gaze softened slightly.

"When we first began speaking of such things, you claimed to have never given much thought to spiritual matters. Why is that?"

"What do you want from me, old man?" Raldus challenged, the last of his patience nearly gone.

"I want you to answer my question."

"There's no point to this!" the warrior declared as he shot to his feet. Pain shot through him from the quick movement, but he ignored the throbbing in his sides as he stared down at the stubborn old goat.

"Do you fear the answer?"

That got him to place his hands on the table and lean toward the old man who showed no sign of being intimidated.

"I fear nothing," Raldus growled.

"Then answer the question."

He glared into Jerald's eyes, but his accuser calmly sat there and met his gaze in a way that both infuriated and disarmed the young warrior. The temptation to beat the arrogance out of the elder was strong, but he would not be provoked into attacking the weak. He could leave, yet that would mean admitting defeat, which was also beyond consideration.

"I can take care of myself and don't need anything from a so-called higher power, so there's no reason to think about such things," he insisted.

"Do you still feel that way?"

"Stop with the questions and make your point."

"These supposed gods and goddesses had no impact on your life whether you worshiped them or not, and you thought your death was a long way off. Now you've learned that it could happen at any moment. Only a fool is unchanged by such an experience, and you are no fool,"

Jerald explained, and Raldus slowly sat down again. This was the first time the old man had ever complimented him in any way, much less regarding his intelligence.

"I don't know how they defeated me," he admitted, his voice quiet and thoughtful.

"Or how you are still alive?" Jerald added, and Raldus gave a single, slow nod as confirmation.

"Those are good questions, and many answers will present themselves to you as truths, but not all of them can be. Do not dismiss what we offer simply because it is different," the abbot stated, then picked up his quill and returned to his work in clear indication the conversation was over.

Grass and dirt blew into Ariela's face as she ran across the field, weighed down by the cauldron she carried by the handle with both hands, its contents protected by a heavy lid. Each gust carried with it the scent of rain as her tan dress billowed behind her, along with the lengths of her dark hair which had escaped from under the white bandanna.

Lightning split the sky and thunder rumbled, rattling the barn walls as she rushed through the main door, sighing in relief as she paused to catch her breath. The clouds had rolled in that morning behind a hot wind, sending the farmers scrambling from the fields to secure the animals, a task which prevented them from coming in for the noonday meal.

Her father and brother were calming a horse spooked by that last roll of thunder. When it settled back down, Raldus stepped around from the other side to rub the mare's gray nose while speaking soothingly.

"Hot soup," she revealed herself, speaking loud enough to be heard above the snorting of the animals but also quietly and calmly to avoid setting them off again.

"That sounds absolutely wonderful," her father, Imri, responded as he and Tobias walked up to her. She set the cauldron on a table near the door, pulled out three bowls from a thin sling across her chest, then ladled the thick broth into them as the rain finally started to fall. The other men kept pitching fresh hay into the stalls or filling troughs, then took turns working as their wives and/or mothers arrived with their meals.

Raldus watched Ariela from his position by the mare, continuing to soothe her instead of coming to get something to eat, so Ariela brought a bowl to him and set to stroking the horse's nose in his place when he took it from her.

"What happened to your horse?" she asked, using her tone to further soothe the horse while addressing Raldus. Lightning flashed and thunder rumbled again, causing the mare to snort and whinny, but she quickly settled thanks to their presence.

"I couldn't afford a horse of my own," the warrior responded between mouthfuls.

"I thought you traveled to help people in dangerous situations?"

"The army does a good job of keeping things safe, for the most part. People like me usually do the jobs too small to be worth their time."

"What about what you were doing when you got hurt?"

The warrior paused and stared at his half empty bowl as the memory of his ordeal took hold. She feared she'd crossed a line with that last question, but said nothing else and focused on the mare as he thought.

"This bandit started out robbing travelers, then moved on to raiding camps and farmsteads as he gathered followers. He always moved out of an area before soldiers arrived and nobody could figure out where he would go next. Then the Esberans started acting more aggressively, causing the senate to send more troops, so they placed a bounty on the bandit to supplement the remaining garrison," he finally explained.

"Esberans?"

"A desert people bordering the republic on the east. Their arrogance knows no bounds even after several massive defeats at Naeran hands."

"So that's when you went after him," she clarified, and he nodded in the affirmative.

"What happened when you found him?" she asked next. He looked at her sternly, then drank the last of the broth and handed the bowl to her before walking away.

She watched him as he strode over to the cow pens and started throwing in some fresh hay, wondering if she should apologize, but then thought better of it and returned to her father and brother instead. When Imri handed over his bowl, she noticed an odd look in his eyes she'd never seen before, but he said nothing and simply returned to work with Tobias at his side, so she just gathered the things and went up to the door.

Now all she had to do was get back to the house through that downpour.

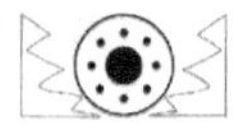

The deepening night was of no concern as Raldus made his way back to the monastery, focusing most of his energy on not wincing in pain with every step. He had spent the day helping the townspeople clean up after yesterday's storm, and his still healing ribs were protesting the entire time. However, he knew that the only way to regain his strength was to push through the pain, and he felt indebted to these people.

There was someone standing at the base of the stairs leading up the hill atop which the monastery sat, and as he drew closer, he recognized it to be Ariela still in her tan linen dress and dark black hair bound up for work despite the late hour.

"Good evening," he greeted, and she echoed the words, but with an air of unease.

"Are you in any pain?" she asked, clearly stalling.

"No," he lied, and waited for her to continue.

She took a deep breath, then said, "There's something I want to show you. Will you come with me?"

He nodded his agreement and followed as she led him back toward the houses, then past them and to the northern wall against which were set some boxes. This was a curious change of habit, but he didn't ask any questions, not even when his curiosity tripled at her climbing up on the boxes then to the top of the wall.

She looked down at him, her countenance inviting him to follow as a gleeful smile broke through her usual calm restraint. All his fatigue and pain evaporated with that one look, and he climbed up after her.

Once they were over, she led him into the woods, at which point he grew a little concerned about possible danger, but she had clearly done this many times before, so he shrugged it off and kept pace beside her.

A few minutes later, they stepped out of the trees to the banks of a small pond, the dark water of which was a black pit under the cloud-covered sky. The pond had swollen from the rain, but there was still plenty of room for them between it and the trees, and the soft grass had prevented the ground from becoming too muddy.

"I like to come here to think sometimes," Ariela sighed as she sat upon a large rock and gazed over the water. He didn't respond at first, and simply followed her gaze and took in the sights. He breathed deep, savoring the smell of damp earth which revitalized both body and mind.

"What is currently in your thoughts?" he asked after a few minutes of silence, which was interrupted only by the chirping of insects and croaking of frogs.

"After Mother died, all that mattered was taking care of Father and Tobias. I gave little thought to the world outside our walls during that time. Now that it has come to us, to me, I wonder how my life has changed and if it will continue to do so."

He looked down at her as she continued staring at the water with unseeing eyes. The implication that he had changed their lives in some significant fashion was a startling revelation. He was certainly grateful for all they had done for him and wanted to return that kindness as best he could while he waited to finish healing, but he'd never considered what their lives had been like before nor what his presence had done to change them.

There was also the discovery that she had been caring for her family as a mother would since she was a child. His own mother had died while pregnant with what would have been his only sibling, and his father never remarried. As a healthy firstborn male in Stoneforge, he spent his childhood in training where they learned to care for themselves. Since his father was also a warrior, it had never occurred to him that he might need someone to help him.

Now as he looked down at this young woman, he took everything she'd done for him and multiplied it across the years to get an idea of what she'd done for her family and community, he realized she possessed a considerable strength hidden within her small frame.

"My mother also died when I was young," he admitted, causing her to snap her gaze up to meet his own with her eyes wide.

"Who took care of you?"

"Self-reliance is a crucial element in our training."

"You were already training?"

His only response was an affirming nod.

"Your whole life has been spent learning to fight?"

Another nod.

Her jaw dropped at this news, then she clenched it shut again and looked back at the water.

"I can't imagine devoting one's entire life to violence," she confessed.

"It is for the same reason as to why you work so hard; to protect and provide for our families," he explained. The code centered on a warrior's duty to home and family, but he chose not to speak on that or admit that he never really understood why that was until now.

"That's not the only reason. Our Lord teaches us to have love for all people and serve them in his name."

That statement so closely resembled what he was just thinking about the code that it took him a moment to consider the implications of that similarity. He looked back over the water to the trees on the other side as he processed those thoughts and feelings, which he then muttered to himself.

"Perhaps we're not so different after all."

Chapter Ten
Escalation

"What happened to you?" Tallio demanded of the filthy man slinking into camp in the middle of the afternoon, his tunic hanging off him in tattered rags. A gust of wind blew past the man into Tallio's face and his nose wrinkled at the sour stench of grime, sweat, and smoke.

"We were attacked. They killed everyone and burned the whole camp," the wretch explained as Tallio stepped around him until he was upwind.

"Who?"

"Soldiers led by Stoneforge Warriors."

Every muscle in Tallio's body tensed at the news, and he stepped closer to speak, forgetting why he was keeping his distance until forced to hold his breath to keep from gagging. It wasn't uncommon for the type of scum that followed him to go days or weeks without bathing, not that he was much better about the routine himself, but he'd grown accustomed to the resulting smell long ago. This was on another level entirely.

"Tell me exactly what they did," he demanded, his voice straining from the effort.

"They came in the night, killing those on watch without making a sound. Then they stormed into the camp, cutting men down before they could grab their weapons. We didn't get any of them."

"You survived."

"They let me go."

The leader glared at him a moment, then dismissed him with a jerk of his head, sending him running off toward the others around the fire, most of which took a step back as he approached.

"Is there a problem?" a deeply accented voice asked from behind, and Tallio stifled a groan before turning to face the large man in polished blue metal armor. Did he ever wear anything else?

"You heard him."

"Yes, but I do not understand your apprehension."

Now Tallio closed the distance and looked up into his face, practically shouting his next statement.

"We aren't ready for this! If the senate is desperate enough to hire Stoneforge Warriors, then they are out to destroy us!"

"Have you not already defeated one of these men and grown in power from that victory? Do it again," the observer remarked. His piercing blue eyes bore into the bandit leader's own, betraying no emotion as his gaze penetrated into the shorter man's very soul.

His failure to intimidate this pompous cretin did not deter Tallio as he held up a single finger to the man's face.

"One. We killed one dumb boy, but even he killed four of my men and hurt many others before we brought him down."

"I see," the observer responded, then stared at the bandit until he lowered his hand and took a step back.

"I never expected those prudish senators to approve the expense, at least not this soon," Tallio confessed.

"Are these warriors really so fearsome?"

The bandit's response was a slow nod, after which he remarked, "I'm surprised you haven't heard about them with all your preparations."

"A single band of mercenaries is not worth our time when there is an entire nation with which to contend."

“Their fame is widespread, and even the senate hesitates to anger them.”

“Very well. I will help you destroy them. Prepare your men to attack their home.”

“Did you not hear me say that even the senate with its massive army fears them?”

“My power far exceeds that of your senate,” the observer sneered.

Tallio looked around the camp as he considered the idea, unable to resist a tiny smile when someone dumped a bucket of water on the recent arrival. The pitiful creature then shouted and screamed as two men proceeded to restrain him while a woman scrubbed him down with a coarse brush.

These men and boys who had joined him were tough, but none of them had received training anywhere near Stoneforge standards, and only a few had ever served in the army. He knew the observer’s people had the means to inflict incredible destruction, but that was still no guarantee.

“No. That would make us into too much of a threat, and even Esbera would become little more than a nuisance in comparison. They would send everything they have against us,” he finally concluded.

“Do you intend to do nothing?”

To do nothing at all wasn’t an option either, as that would be admitting defeat and he might as well send everyone home. Then an idea came to him, prompting a devious smile as the details unfolded.

“We will attack and destroy the camp of those who did this. That will be enough for now.”

The night slowly retreated as over thirty bandits gathered at the bottom of the hill where the warriors were encamped. Tallio stood behind a tree with the observer, leaning out only enough to watch his men sneak into position through the brush and keep an eye on the two soldiers at the top of the hill.

It took them two days to find the camp belonging to those who had destroyed his own, and another three to gather enough men to outnumber its occupants two-to-one. His initial concerns had faded behind the growing anger brought on by another raid against him, this time on one of his patrols, and the realization that victory here would swell his reputation and numbers. Even now, men were coming from foreign lands to fight for him, and they often brought their women to contribute to the cooking and mending of clothes for the entire camp to which they belonged.

The Naeran senate and its false representation of the people in a quest to create and preserve true civilization was at an end. It was time to empower the people by allowing them to act as they chose, and letting the strong take charge instead of forcing them to tolerate the weak.

It remained gloomy under the trees as the day continued to brighten, keeping them hidden, but the camp guards had gone from mere shadows to fully visible men with spears and tower shields. His men were in position, so Tallio nodded to his archers, two of whom took careful aim before loosing their arrows.

A strike to the neck caused one guard to drop his spear as he stumbled backward and fell to the ground. The other screamed when the arrow hit him in the knee, then he fell to his side and rolled down the hill with his spear bouncing along behind him.

"Now!" Tallio shouted, and his bandits surged out of the trees, yelling as they went. Their leader and the observer jogged up behind them, the former halting long enough to slash the throat of the fallen guard before running up the hill.

He expected to find his bandits slaughtering soldiers and warriors as they crawled from their tents, but upon cresting the hill he instead saw several men in loincloths bearing swords and shields fighting back. Many of the attackers were already dead or dying at their feet.

Even worse, the guards in their leather armor had rushed in from the other sides and were forming up around the ragtag bandits, attempting to pen them in while the warriors finished them off.

"Pull back!" Tallio ordered, and his men either turned and ran or backpedaled until reaching him, at which point they formed up around him.

The defenders formed a line beside their tents, the six warriors in nothing but loincloths taking the middle while the six soldiers split up to take the sides.

"You might as well give up now, vermin," the warrior with the short black beard sprinkled with white declared from the center.

Tallio said nothing as his eyes darted all over to take in the scene. At least ten of his men lay on the ground, writhing in pain or not moving at all, nearly eliminating his number advantage. The distance between the two sides was such that his archers would only be able to get off a single volley before the warriors closed the distance, and there was always the chance their shields would block the arrows.

A chuckle interrupted his frantic thinking, and he focused on the enemy line to see most of the warriors smiling gleefully, while a few of the younger ones were even snickering. His blood boiled at the sight, but even he knew better than to let it get him killed in a foolhardy tantrum.

"Give up and some of you may yet live. Fight, and you all die."

"I was just thinking the same thing about you," Tallio shot back, his words causing several of the warriors to burst out in full-on laughter.

"Have it your way," the warrior commander relented and gave the order to advance.

All out of options, Tallio looked to the observer, who was currently watching him studiously. When their eyes met, he nodded, then stepped to the front of their line and held up his staff as the defenders kept marching toward them.

Then with a sound unlike anything ever heard before, the closest description he could fathom being of wood cracking in the fire but much louder, a beam of red light shot out from the staff head toward the warrior commander. It burned right through his shield, striking him in the chest and sending him flying backward to land on the ground with a smoking hole where his heart used to be.

The soldiers jumped back in surprise, but the warriors let out a war cry and charged forward. Two more of them fell to the staff's power before they could reach its wielder, but the bandits swarmed in as he stepped back.

Taking heart from the courage of the warriors, the soldiers threw their spears into the melee, most of which skewered a bandit through the chest, then drew their swords and ran in. The observer shot one of them down before they could close the distance, the beam slicing through the leather armor as easily as the wooden shields.

He took aim to let off another shot, but a bandit fell backward into him, which sent the beam arcing across the camp, scorching the ground and setting two tents on fire.

Tallio grabbed the bandit and threw him back into the fight, then dodged a sword swung at his midsection. He grabbed the offending soldier by the wrist, pulled him off-balance, then slid his own sword over the shield to stab him below the throat.

A warrior managed to get through the throng to threaten the observer, but his target casually side-stepped while using his staff to trip the man in the same motion. While he was down, the observer burned a hole through his back to ensure he never threatened anyone again.

It suddenly grew silent, and Tallio looked around to discover that was the last of them. Less than ten of his own men remained, but they were victorious.

"Get what you can as fast as you can!" Tallio shouted to his surviving men.

The burning tents spew smoke into the air, choking those present along with the stench of blood and burnt flesh. None of this bothered the bandits as they rushed into the camp to grab whatever they could find, except for one who set to work relieving the dead soldiers of their gear.

"This is the end of your days as simple bandits. You are ready for the next step," the observer stated from Tallio's right.

"What are you yapping about?" the bandit responded, too tired to play this man's games.

"You wish to rule this land, do you not?"

"That is the promise your people made me."

"That will not be achieved by hiding in the countryside, stealing what you need and constantly moving to avoid capture."

"Speak plainly or not at all."

"It is time you established a fortified position and stable means of production. It would also be wise to train your men and make them into a proper army."

"These are peasants, not soldiers. Many of them were already rejected for service in the Naeran army. This is all that can be expected of them."

"Their inability to become something more is your failure, not theirs," the observer remarked and Tallio turned to face him, gripping his sword tight but not raising it.

"Watch how you speak to me. I don't care who you are or what your people have done for me; I won't be spoken to in that manner," he threatened, but the observer only looked down at him with an amused grin.

"My attitude toward you will not change by you acting even more foolish. It is your responsibility to mold those who follow you into what you require. People are only as good as those who lead them."

Tallio considered lopping off the man's head, or at least bloodying that arrogant face, but chose to take a step back instead.

"They are not soldiers," he repeated.

"They will serve our purposes. The Naerans are weak. You have proven that. The Esberans are weakening them further. It will not take much to defeat them," the observer explained. He had a point, but Tallio wasn't about to admit that.

A smirk replaced his angry glare as an idea occurred to him, and he told the other man he knew the perfect place to take over.

"Move out!" he shouted at his men after taking another glance at the sun.

Tired of staring at maps and sloppy lists of men serving him, Tallio stormed out of his tent and stomped toward the fire in the center of camp in search of something to eat. His head felt like it was about to explode from all he had to remember, prompting memories of the headaches he'd endured when his patrons forced him to learn to read and write. Fortunately, the image of meat still sizzling after coming straight off the campfire spit pushed aside all else as his stomach grumbled in anticipation.

Yet as he walked, he couldn't help but notice how quiet it was and those of his men who saw him cast a furtive glance before quickly pretending to be busy.

An odd state of affairs for a bunch of miscreants, especially when they'd just defeated a group of the best warriors in any of the known lands. Curious, he slowed his approach and came up behind a pair of men sitting on wooden stools near the fire, careful to conceal his presence despite having to get close to discern their whispers.

"No one has," the one on the right said in response to something said before Tallio was close enough.

"How can light do that?"

"That wasn't just light."

"What else was it?"

"How would I know?"

"You're the one who said it was something else!"

"That doesn't mean I know what it is!"

The two grew quiet as they picked at the meat on wooden plates held in one hand while staring at the fire. They were clearly talking about the observer and his weapon, which Tallio supposed he should have known would be a problem despite his own familiarity with such things.

"What kind of man can wield such a weapon?" the bandit on the left, the younger of the two, continued his questioning.

"Who could make something like that is a better question."

"Only the gods have such power," the young man observed, earning a derisive snort from his companion.

"That man is no god."

"He could be their servant."

"And why would they send him to us? We're hardly worthy of their favor."

The younger bandit's response was so quiet that Tallio almost couldn't hear it above the crackling of the fire.

"It could have been Olorin. What if we're doing the work of evil?"

"Enough!" Tallio proclaimed, the sudden declaration from so close behind causing the men to shoot to their feet, dropping their plates and knocking over their stools in the process.

"Boss! We...," the older one started to say.

"Save it," Tallio demanded as he walked around them, after which he turned to face them with the fire behind him. He looked around at the others gathered there to make sure he had their full attention, then settled on the two he'd been observing to address them directly.

"The stranger is not your concern. Where he comes from is not important. No god controls us. We make our own way, and there is nothing evil about that," he told them, looking at the younger man in particular at the last point.

"Yes, boss!" both men echoed.

The bandit leader glared at them, then took another look at the others. He could tell that each one of them was afraid, and their eyes only grew wider when he met their gaze, showing their fear was of him and no one else.

Satisfied, Tallio grabbed a plate of steaming venison and stalked off back to his tent.

Chapter Eleven

Heart of the Warrior

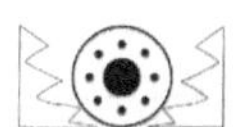

For today's midday meal, Raldus had agreed to meet Keid in the small park on the west side of the monastery plaza. It was doubtless going to be another lecture on belief, which had been growing in frequency this past month, the fifth since his arrival. The monk seemed determined to convert him before he left them, an earnestness which kept growing as he healed.

Upon stepping off the stone brick stairs coming up from the town, he saw several monks whispering earnestly and hurrying toward the gate. Concerned, he increased his own pace and followed, and soon heard raised voices and saw a crowd gathered around the entrance to the community.

"You are in republic lands and you will heed the senate's order!"

"We have nothing to give!"

Raldus nudged his way to the front of the group where he was surprised to see Jerald standing before a senate deputy in his white toga with a blue sash and a retinue of six guards. The guards wore steel breastplates, leather cingulum, and carried a spear while a sword hung from their left hip, but they did not have helmets or shields.

"I think you're lying," the deputy accused.

"How dare you accuse me of such a thing!" Jerald retorted.

"I'm done arguing with you, old man," the deputy declared before tilting his head to the right to address his soldiers, "Search the place and seize everything of value!"

The monks gasped in fear as the guards stepped toward Jerald to shove him aside, but Raldus moved to block their way.

"Hold!" he shouted, knowing the assertive tone would cause them to hesitate. Everyone present froze and stared at Raldus as he held up his hands chest high and palms forward to appear unthreatening.

"I will not allow you to harm these people."

"What are you going to do about it?"

His only response to that was to turn his right forearm for them to see the tattoo of a shield between cliffs. The soldiers had lowered their spears in anticipation of an assault, but now raised them and took a step back to appear as unthreatening as possible, earning them a disgusted look from the deputy.

"If they say they don't have anything to give, then there is nothing for you here," Raldus insisted as he lowered his hands.

"It's your fault we're having to do this! You and the rest of your kind!" the deputy shouted.

"How?"

"All those rates and expenses you demand just to stop a rabble of bandits!"

"Why pay us to do this? Where is the army?"

The deputy paused as confusion mixed with his angry expression.

"Where have you been the last three months?"

"I was injured on a job and these people were kind enough to give me care and shelter."

"Do any of you people ever leave this place?" the deputy questioned as he looked around at the monks with a sense of realization creeping into his expression.

"Not as much as we should," Keid spoke up, surprising Raldus with his presence, although he should have known the man was never far from trouble.

"I'm more interested in learning how you even knew we were here," Jerald interjected as he cast an accusing glare at Raldus, who chose to ignore it.

"Did you really think we don't know every inch of our territory?"

"You've never bothered us before."

"It wasn't worth our time. Things change."

"What is happening?" Raldus pressed.

"The problems in Esbera have erupted into war, forcing us to send more legions. The northern tribes have also increased their aggression, with one even being so bold as to cross the sea and attack fishing camps on our side. With the local garrisons depleted, the bandits causing trouble over the past year have increased their own attacks. That is what you warriors are supposed to be resolving."

"So the senate has levied new taxes to pay for our services," Raldus concluded, and the deputy nodded his confirmation.

"Taxes we are incapable of paying," Jerald asserted.

"That's not my problem. I will not leave here empty-handed, no matter how fiercely your little dog here growls."

The soldiers gripped their spears tighter and glanced at each other behind the deputy's back. They were much better equipped and trained than those bandits who had nearly killed Raldus, but they were also smarter and knew that not all of them would survive a fight with him, especially given the mischievous smile he was giving them as his blood surged in anticipation.

"Are you going to be the first to attack me?" Raldus teased, causing the deputy to look back at his guards and finally notice their anxiety.

"What's the matter with you? There's six of you and he's not even armed!"

"I saw a Stoneforge warrior fight in the arena once. He demolished everyone and everything he faced," the officer commented.

"I remember that fight. He didn't even let them pay him for it. Said he was just doing it for the training," another soldier spoke up.

"You are Naeran soldiers, and you will remove this whelp from my path now!"

There was a brief hesitation, but then the soldiers lowered their spears again and began advancing toward Raldus. Most of the monks backed away from him while Jerald continued to stand in front of the deputy.

"Surely there's a way we can resolve this without violence!" Keid implored as he stepped up to stand beside Raldus with his hands held up at chest level.

"I agree," Raldus added, and the soldiers stopped with spear tips mere feet from his chest.

"What do you suggest?" Jerald asked as the deputy fumed beside him.

"I will serve as these people's tribute and fight these bandits without any fee."

The guard officer looked over his shoulder for a cue from the deputy who scowled back at him. The man clearly didn't enjoy having his authority challenged, but they could only hope he wasn't stupid enough to force the fight merely to assuage his ego.

"So be it. Report to the capital forthwith. Guards!" he finally consented, then spun around and exited through the gate with his retinue following.

The monks let out a sigh of relief and began muttering amongst themselves as Jerald and Keid both came up to Raldus.

"Are you sure this is for the best? You aren't yet fully healed," Keid prompted.

"I'm healed enough."

"You do not have to fight for us," Jerald told him in a kind tone the warrior had never heard him use before.

"I have to finish this fight eventually. Now is as good a time as any," Raldus stated, then walked off to go gather his things.

The door to the house opened, causing Ariela to startle at the sound and spill the soup she was carrying. Imri and Tobias entered and glanced at her as she hastily set the pot on the table, then grabbed a towel to clean up the mess.

The two of them took their seats, having already washed up outside, and waited patiently as she fetched the bread and added it to the table, then filled their bowls with soup and cups with tea.

Then the door opened again, and she nearly dropped the clay tea pitcher as Uncle Nurin and Keid entered.

"Are we interrupting?" Nurin asked politely.

"No, we were just getting started. Would you like to lead the prayer?" Imri responded.

"Certainly," Keid agreed in his role as the senior monk in the room. Ariela hurriedly brought each of them a bowl and cup, filled them up, then stood aside as Keid blessed the food. When he finished, all three of them took their seats.

"I'm pleased to share our evening meal with you. What brings you here tonight?" Imri remarked.

"We've grown accustomed to having a guest these past months. It feels a little strange to think he'll be leaving us in the morning, probably never to return," Nurin answered.

"Yes. More's the pity that he leaves without having accepted the salvation of our Lord," Keid added.

"That is his choice," Imri remarked. Ariela suddenly realized that she'd been missing her soup when she'd gone to dip her spoon into it and covered up her blunder by tearing off a piece of bread.

"Of course, but it's a shame he won't have the chance to learn more," Keid continued.

"He may yet be convinced if only he heard something with which he connects," Nurin expounded.

The conversation ceased for a time, with the only sound being the dipping of spoons in wooden bowls and the slurping of soup. Ariela kept her eyes down, knowing it was not her place to express her own concerns or feelings.

"I wonder if he's healed enough to do this," Keid brought up.

"He works with us just fine," Imri retorted, his voice betraying a growing annoyance.

"Farm work and combat are entirely different things, Brother."

"In one, you can work slowly and still get the job done. With the other, a single wrong move ends your life," Keid added.

"I'm sure he knows what he's doing," Imri insisted.

"What do you think, Ariela?" Nurin suddenly asked. She froze in place, then slowly looked up to see the monks looking at her while Imri continued to eat. Tobias had finished his meal and was watching with keen interest.

She caught her father's eye, who nodded his permission for her to speak, and she finally asked, "What do you mean?", her voice sounding small and weak.

"You are responsible for his care. Do you think he's healed enough to fight?" Keid pressed. She glanced from one man to the next, her thoughts racing faster than she could process them.

"I don't know," she confessed after looking down at the floor.

"How has he been doing? Do his injuries still bother him?" Nurin questioned.

"He's strong, but he still feels pain at times. It's hard to be sure because he tries to hide it."

No one said anything this time, and upon looking up, she saw they were all finished, so she got up and began clearing the table.

"Perhaps it would be for the best if you went with him," Keid suggested, causing her to nearly drop the dishes, but she managed to make it to the washbasin.

"I can't leave my father and brother," she declined without turning around.

"We would look after them and provide any assistance they might need," Keid offered.

"They need me."

"You've always found time to help us at the monastery, even with all your duties here. We can and should return the favor, especially when a man's soul is at stake."

"What about Tobias?"

"He's old enough to look after himself now," Nurin assured.

She couldn't think of any other objections, so she slowly turned around and looked to her father for his say.

"Do you want to keep helping him?"

She could only nod in response.

No one said anything, and she looked at the floor again to await his judgement.

Then she heard a chair scrape the floor, his heavy footsteps coming toward her, and finally felt his hand on her chin lifting up to bring her eyes to meet his own.

"You are far more than a man could ever ask for in a daughter. Your depths of compassion and strength are immeasurable, and I am proud of the woman you've become."

Her eyes watered and a few tears snuck down her face, and he reached up with his other hand to wipe them away with his thumb.

"I'm not blind to what you've come to feel. Do not worry about us. This is your time. Follow your heart, for that is how Rosjen leads us all," he encouraged as his own eyes grew misty.

She gave him a big hug and said, "I love you, Father," and he returned it with his head resting upon hers.

After they separated, the others joined them and Keid led them in a prayer for her safety and wisdom.

"Be safe," Tobias told her, and she gave him a quick hug around the shoulders before turning back to the dishes.

"No. We will take care of that. You go and pack what you will need and get some rest. You'll need it," Nurin insisted.

"I should still finish my chores while I'm here."

"He's right, Ariela. Go," Imri directed, and Keid proved their sincerity by rolling up his sleeves before plunging his hands into the dishwater.

She finally accepted their offer with a smile and hurried to her room as a list of anything she might need rushed through her head.

A deep anxiety disrupted her focus as it sank in just how far from home she was about to go.

What had she gotten herself into?

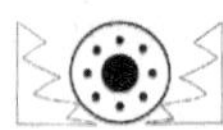

Once he was sure he had everything he would need, Raldus tied the burlap bag shut with a white cord, then stood and threw it over his right shoulder, careful not to hit anything in the small room. The town's supply runner had offered to let him borrow his horse, but he had refused. These people had already given more than he could ever imagine, and there was no telling if he would be able to return it.

The sun was lightening the sky when he stepped out of the monastery's main building into the already warm summer air. He descended the steps and started toward the gate, but stopped when he saw the abbot approaching along with a boy in the white robes of an initiate who was carrying a leather bundle in both arms.

"This is for you," Jerald revealed. The initiate held out the bundle toward him, the movement causing the familiar clink of metal on metal.

"No, you've already done enough for me."

"We have no use for this, but you do," Jerald insisted in an all too familiar authoritative tone, so Raldus set down his bag and accepted the bundle, setting it on the bricks between them to inspect its contents.

"Where did you get all this?" he asked. Inside was a full set of legion armor and a sword, all of it well-maintained and shining in the dawn light.

"In my youth, a soldier fled a cruel commander. When they pursued him, he tried to hide in the forest but became lost and found his way here. We sheltered him, and eventually stored away his gear when he chose to convert and stay."

"It has been in storage all this time?" Raldus questioned, the disbelief clear in his tone.

"The abbot at the time chose to bless it as a holy relic, to be preserved and kept from being used to cause harm until such time it was needed to serve and protect," Jerald explained.

"It was also said for it to be given to one who could be trusted to use it only in defense of the weak," a familiar voice said from behind, and Raldus turned to see Keid standing there with hands clasped inside his sleeves. The monk smiled kindly at him as he sheathed the sword again and held it by the scabbard in his left hand.

"You think that's me?"

"Without a doubt."

The warrior turned toward Jerald, who nodded his agreement. He then stepped back to where he could see both monks and held the sword up in the palms of his hands.

"I thank you for this gift and shall endeavor to be worthy," he vowed, then placed everything back in the bundle, tied it to the sack, and tossed both over his shoulder.

"God be with you," Keid told him. Jerald's farewell was only a stiff nod which betrayed no emotion. With nothing else to say or do, Raldus gave a curt nod to each of them in turn, and marched off through the gate.

Chapter Twelve

On The Road

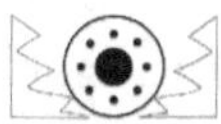

The more he walked, the more Raldus' old life and strength returned to him. It had only been an hour, but it was already feeling as if the past few months were nothing but a dream and he was now waking up to resume his purpose in life. All his training as a child and the experiences of the past three years since leaving home played through his mind. With each step, a different memory appeared, his muscles loosened a little more, and soon he was standing tall even with the added weight of his supplies.

As he walked along the seldom traveled path, the isolation drew him ever deeper into his thoughts. It dawned on him that this supposed dream had permanently transformed him, leaving no chance of returning to his former self. He could not say what had changed, only that he wasn't sure he still wanted the fame and glory which he'd sought his entire life.

Where did that leave him now?

A sound from behind snapped him from his thoughts, and he froze in place to listen. He couldn't hear anything now except the normal sounds of the forest, such as the squirrel jumping from tree to tree to his left, but he was certain what had stopped him was not a natural sound.

He turned and scanned the path behind him, a path which one could tell was normally overgrown, but was clear now because of the deputy's party coming and going in the previous days. There was still nothing to see, hear, or smell, but he couldn't shake the feeling he was being watched.

"I know someone is there. Reveal yourself," he called out.

There was no answer, and he slowly crouched to set his gear on the ground, then reached for the knife on his right ankle, having not yet equipped the sword given him by the monks.

A rustling behind a tree grabbed his attention and a moment later, Ariela timidly stepped out onto the path. She was dressed for work like any other time he'd seen her, with a light brown dress cinched tight with a belt around her waist, leather sandals, and her dark hair tied up under a white bandanna, but the sack over her left shoulder indicated her travel plans.

"What are you doing here?" he growled as he replaced the knife and stood to face her.

"I was worried about you being alone and wanted to help," she replied in a small voice as she stared at the ground.

"I can take care of myself. Go home," he commanded as he pointed a finger at the path behind her.

"You are not yet restored from your injuries," she insisted, having now gathered the courage to look up at him.

"That is no longer your concern."

"I want to make sure you are well - and safe."

"You are not safe out here. Go home!" he asserted, his voice rising.

She didn't speak, or move, but only looked at him with the kindness he'd come to expect from her, but also with a determination he did not recognize. Realizing that his force of will would not be enough to get her to turn back, he lowered his hand and stepped closer to speak in a softer tone.

"The things I have told you about this world are only a small part of what you might encounter and reveal nothing about what I will have to face and do. You will see people hurt and killed, and some will attempt to do things to you, possibly unspeakable things. Some of them will even approach you as a friend before doing what they want with you. Go home and fear not such evil," he described in as much detail as he dared.

He looked into her eyes as she reflected upon his words, and saw fear threaten her sweet innocence, but it did not displace the kindness or determination.

"What manner of people are we if we do not take care of one another?" she eventually asked in a voice so low as to be little more than a whisper.

While looking into her eyes, he realized that she would not be persuaded to leave him. He could take her back, but what would stop her from following again?

"You stay close to me and follow my instructions to the letter. Understood?" he demanded with a finger held up to her face. She nodded once in agreement, then he retrieved his bag and began walking once more.

Neither of them spoke, and now his thoughts focused on whether she would actually be any help or nothing but a burden.

"Wow," Ariela breathed upon exiting the forest path beside Raldus, who also paused as she took in the sight bathed in the orangish glow of the sun which had sunk low in the sky.

The trees had an opening cut through them, which was over thirty feet wide and stretching as far as they could see to the east and west. In the middle of this opening, there was a wide road of white stone bricks with a small ditch on either side.

"You didn't know about this?" Raldus questioned from where he stood in front of her and to the right. He was also looking around, but his eyes were sharp and alert rather than filled with awe.

“Our supply runners have spoken of it, but I never imagined it was this large. What it must have taken to build such a thing,” she marveled.

He glanced at her, then immediately went back to looking around as if expecting something to jump out at them at any moment.

“I met him before leaving, but at first I thought he was no more than a quartermaster. He did say that he goes out for supplies a few times a year, but I was under the impression you produced everything you need yourselves,” he confessed.

“There are some things we need that we can’t produce ourselves, such as metal for the blacksmith to fashion new tools,” she explained, to which he nodded his understanding.

She looked west, opposite the direction she knew they would be taking. To the east was a town where their runners conducted business, but the west was a complete mystery to her.

“Where does it go?”

“To another country called Kostrai, a land bordering the ocean and filled with barely civilized tribals.”

“Are they dangerous?” she questioned, her voice breaking a little as she remembered why they were here.

“No. We have nothing to fear from them,” Raldus assured her as he looked east, toward the setting sun.

“We should camp here tonight. It’s too far to the nearest inn.”

“I’ll set up while you gather firewood,” Ariela offered as she lowered her bag to the ground.

“No fire, and not here,” he declared as he turned back to the path and reentered the forest, forcing her to heave the bag back to her shoulder and hurry after him.

A few yards into the woods, he turned off the path and found a small clearing between some trees deep enough to be unseen from either the road or path.

“Why not make a fire?” she questioned as she set the sack down again.

"Someone might see it," he insisted after putting down his own bag and setting to clearing away ground clutter with his sandaled foot.

"I thought you said we were safe?"

"I said the Kostrai aren't dangerous, not that we are safe," he clarified. Satisfied there was enough space for them now, he knelt down to untie the bedroll from the top of his sack and she did the same with hers.

It was sure to be warm enough as it was mid-summer, but the light would have been comforting, yet it made sense that they didn't know who else was out here or what might happen if they were discovered.

As they worked, she found herself acutely aware of every little sound around them. Her heart raced as every rustling of leaves or small animal scurrying through the brush suddenly became a bandit sneaking up on them. Some of these sounds were so loud that she glanced at Raldus, expecting him to be ready to fight something, but each time he didn't react to it, which helped her to calm down again.

When she finished with her bedroll, she pulled out a towel then stood looking all around them, wondering where she could find a source of water. It was rather dark under the trees now, but she still needed to wash off the sweat and other grime before trying to sleep.

Her wandering gaze inevitably fell on Raldus, who she discovered was standing there watching her with a questioning expression.

"Is there water nearby?"

He only shook his head in the negative.

"How are we going to wash?"

"We don't."

She stared at him in the hopes he was joking, but he remained completely serious - yet how could he be? Was he really suggesting they try to sleep while sticky and smelly from traveling all day?

"Such is the nature of traveling," he expressed when she just kept standing there. This was clearly how it was going to be, so she sighed and put the towel back in the bag.

"Sit down and I'll check on your injuries," she dictated after he confirmed everything was ready for the night.

"I'm fine," he grunted while looking at the ground as if something else remained to be done.

"I'll be the judge of that."

"Leave me alone!" he demanded harshly.

"This is why I'm here. There's still a chance you could have aggravated something, and I'm not going to let that put you at risk of further harm," she insisted, her own voice remaining calm and even.

He looked at her, and even in the deepening gloom, she saw surprise and some respect mixed with his stubborn expression. Her response was to stare back. Where his health was concerned, it didn't matter if he became angry at the fact a woman was defying him, unless he intended to strike her.

Sighing, he glanced around, located an old stump, and sat down. She started by checking his arms and legs, lifting them one at a time to see how they flexed while listening for any pops. The bruising was completely gone now, and his skin was now a lovely shade of brown from his time in the sun practicing combat and helping the farmers.

She spent only a little time on the arms, then moved on to his ribs, which she gave more careful attention, working around his tunic instead of having him take it off. She resisted reacting to the sour stench coming off him, especially with his arms raised, and tried not to think about what he must be thinking about her own scent right now. He winced here and there as she probed them, but they felt strong and the flesh firm to the touch.

"Everything seems to be proceeding normally," she concluded as she stepped away. All he did was grunt as he stood up, go over to his bedroll which he'd placed to the right side of hers, then climb in before drawing his sword from its sheath and placing it on the ground next to him.

She took a deep breath to suppress a sigh, then got into her own bedroll, feeling odd to still be in her dress with hair tied up, but that was better than being out here in nothing but her undergarments.

They sat up long enough to eat a few pieces of bread, cheese, and dried fruit, washing it all down with water from their leather flasks. All of this was done without speaking, leaving the sounds of the soft breeze and that of the nighttime creatures coming out to be their only accompaniment.

When they finally lay down to go to sleep, he did so almost immediately as evidenced by his steady breathing, but she lay there staring at the stars through the canopy, feeling as if she was learning for the first time the true magnitude of the world.

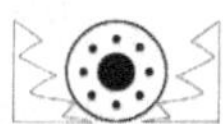

When they broke camp that morning, Raldus had elected to equip his sword rather than repack it, but the armor he left in its bundle so as to not draw too much attention. They had eaten a quick breakfast of bread, cheese, and dried meat, then gotten on the road before the sun rose above the trees.

He was stiff from the day before, a fact which he did his best to hide from his overly concerned companion, and he was grateful when she didn't try to baby him again. This time, his strength and flexibility returned even faster than it had the previous day, showing him that the power he'd known all his life was once again his to command.

It wasn't long before they encountered someone going the other direction, a small group of merchants with a cart full of textiles. He watched them with a hand on his sword as they passed, and they stared at him in kind, but they passed without incident.

They saw more people as the day went on, including a barrel-laden cart going the same way as them, which managed to pass them thanks to being pulled by two horses instead of just one as was the norm. At the end of the first hour, he relaxed enough to not reach for his sword every time, but still watched each fellow traveler with a healthy suspicion.

"Is it always this busy?" Ariela wondered aloud after a family group complete with young children had walked by.

"Yes. Kostrai is a major trading partner of the republic."

"What do you trade?"

The questions she kept asking were of things that everyone should know, a fact which tried his patience at times, but he would just remind himself of how she had grown up in near complete isolation and tell her what she wanted to know. Besides, he had to admit that he had found a certain enjoyment in explaining things and seeing them anew through her eyes.

"They mostly trade salted fish which the army in particular likes to use for campaign rations, but nearly everyone buys to some extent. The republic offers many different things in return, with weapons and armor being among the most common, although the war has probably changed that."

They traveled the rest of the day in that manner, with her asking the occasional question and him answering. At one point, she made a comment about so many people not knowing her god, but he said nothing to that. None of the other travelers attempted to interact with them, nor did they with them.

Other than stopping for about an hour at noon to eat beside the road, they walked the whole day and made swift progress thanks to the road. He had to reduce the pace more than once over the course of the afternoon as she became unable to keep up. He'd learned enough about her life to know that she spent most every day on her feet working, but that didn't mean she was accustomed to walking this far in a single stretch.

Despite having to go a little slower, they reached the fort which guarded the road to the great forest with over an hour of sunlight left in the day. Gray stone walls with evenly spaced towers surrounded the complex while soldiers in shining steel breastplates and bronze-colored helmets watched from the towers and walked the battlements.

Ariela drew in close to him as he confidently walked up to the gate which was wide enough to accommodate four carts side-by-side, and he waited as a guard inspected the cart ahead of them while another stood watch behind him.

When they waved the,cart through, he stepped up to the first guard while Ariela stood behind him.

"What's your business in Republic lands?" the guard demanded in a clipped tone.

Raldus' response was to hold up his right arm to present his Stoneforge tattoo, which the guard gave a quick glance before waving them through.

"This place looks to be around the same size as Our Sacred Refuge, but there are so few people here," Ariela marveled once they were inside, referring to the monastery and town by their combined name.

"The senate probably redeployed many of them to the wars or to watch the other borders since there is so little danger at this one. Most of those who remain are out on patrol."

They passed through the fort and its eastern gate with no further conversation or being stopped again, then made their way to the town a mere ten-minute walk away. The town was busy with travelers looking for a place to stay and residents finishing up their work, but all was clean and orderly as befit any Naeran settlement.

The first thing he did was find the local inn where he bartered a meal and a room for the night, using a roll of fine leather gifted him by the townspeople of Solace since the bandits stole all of his money and his hosts of the past few months didn't use currency. He had tried to refuse the things they gave him to barter, insisting he could live off the land until reaching the city, but they had insisted, saying that they felt they should help him and wanted to do so. Of course, now he knew at least part of that had to be them looking out for Ariela, as they likely knew her plan before he did.

"We'll put our belongings in the room now, but will take the meal after we return from the bathhouse," he informed the owner upon concluding their deal, to which the pudgy, balding man nodded his consent.

"Bathhouse?" Ariela questioned after they'd walked away.

"The name says it all," he replied as they ascended the stairs to the second floor. Upon finding their room, he unlocked it, set his bag down, then stood aside as she lay down her own burden.

"But it's a public place?"

"Yes," he said without disguising his confusion at her discomfort. He was well aware that her people used personal tubs for bathing, much like many Naerans who lived in the countryside, but she'd seen him without clothes many times when tending to his wounds. He'd also seen both the men and women of her community enjoy a leisurely swim in the same pool where they washed their clothes, but they still wore their undergarments on those occasions.

"Other people will be there?"

"Probably, but a bathhouse in a town this size will have different areas for men and women," he tried to assure her, but knew he had failed when she blushed.

She looked away and at the floor, not saying anything else but also not making any move to follow him.

"You're uncomfortable exposing yourself in front of others?" he said as both statement and question, and she nodded in the affirmative without looking up.

"Last night you wanted to wash, but now that you're able to properly bathe, you're going to refuse?"

"No, but...," she said, her voice sounding small and trailing off. Then she took a deep breath and finished the thought, "Couldn't I do so here?"

"No, not really," he replied unsympathetically. Yet she continued to stand there, shuffling back and forth on her feet, until he finally sighed and promised to find a private place for her to wash at the house.

She nodded her consent, then pulled a fresh dress and towel from her sack before following him.

This woman and her people continued to be a mystery to him, one which irritated him and piqued his curiosity at the same time. As they walked, it occurred to him that the way she was acting now that she was in his world must be much the same way he behaved while in hers.

Was it too much for him to treat her with the same patience and respect they had shown him?

Since when did he care one way or the other?

Last night at the inn, Ariela had slept soundly, the unfamiliar sounds doing little to bother her since this time she was clean and filled with a hot meal. It was quite a shock to learn that the Naerans bathed in front of each other every day, and it had clearly frustrated Raldus when she didn't want to do the same. The fact these people were seeing each other naked wasn't the problem, as that happened from time to time, even for her people, but there were some things that should be done in private.

A similar issue arose from there being only one bed in the room, which was wide enough for both of them, yet still quite snug. They agreed to sleep fully clothed, a discussion which revealed that both their cultures had similar views on men and women waiting for marriage to have physical relations. Not that either of them intended to do this, regardless of tradition, but it was always better to avoid temptation.

Now they were on the road again, which was much emptier on this side of the town, a fact which seemed to create a sense of unease in her companion. He had chosen to wear the armor given to him by Jerald and kept looking around as if something was going to jump out at them at any moment. Out of respect, she chose not to speak and instead took in the sights of lush fields which featured far fewer trees than the forest but still had plenty spaced out over the hills, most of them oaks but also the occasional spruce and stand of beech.

Two or three hours after their departure, Raldus suddenly dropped his pack and drew his sword, causing her to stop short just behind him to his left. She followed his gaze to see something up ahead in the ditch on the right, but she couldn't make out what.

"Drop that and stay close to me," he instructed. She set her bag next to his, then stayed a foot or two behind him as he walked up to the object.

Upon drawing closer, she was finally able to see that it was an overturned cart, and shortly after that, a strong metallic scent nearly overpowered her sense of smell. A few more steps revealed a man in the ditch with an arrow in his chest, and she clasped a hand over her mouth to suppress a gasp.

"Wait here," Raldus ordered, so she waited in the road as he walked around the cart, then wandered around in the grass, alert for any danger. She watched him as he stopped to inspect something on the ground, deliberately focusing her attention on him and not staring at the poor man in front of her. When he circled back around to the road further down from the cart, he stopped again to check on something before continuing to the other side.

He sheathed his sword several minutes later and returned to her, calmer now, but with his eyes still darting to all sides and he didn't look at her when he spoke.

"Get the bags and let's go."

"We can't just leave him like that," she protested, looking back down at the man. Although she'd never seen anyone murdered before, she had seen men mutilated and killed in farming accidents and even animals mauled by the occasional predator wily enough to get past their walls.

Now that her initial shock was wearing off, she was remembering the responsibility of every decent human being.

"Whoever did this is gone, but it wasn't that long ago. They may return."

"That doesn't change what we need to do."

"Do you remember agreeing to follow my instructions?" he challenged, locking eyes with her to drive home his point with the fire in his green irises.

"Yes, but I will not leave him like this," she insisted as she defiantly stared back.

They stayed like that for several seconds, during which she observed a multitude of emotions play out across his features. At one point, she feared he might even decide to abandon her there in his anger.

"Bring the packs up here, and be quick about it," he commanded. She didn't obey right away, but he stepped back, took another look around, then knelt over the man and took hold of the arrow shaft.

Realizing that he had chosen to do the right thing, she jogged back to their sacks, then dragged both of them to the cart. By the time she returned, Raldus had removed the arrow, rolled the man onto his back, and crossed his arms over his chest.

"Get a blanket from your kit, wrap him in it, and tie it tight. If at any point you sense something is wrong, cry out as loud as you can," he instructed as he untied his own bag. Her only response was to do as she was told and dig into her sack for one of the spare blankets while he pulled out two blankets of his own.

He walked off into the grass while she set to work covering this man whom she'd never met but whose earthly vessel still deserved her respect. They didn't have any rope to spare, so the best she could do to tie the top and bottom was to fold and tuck the corners into one another.

She was just finishing up when Raldus returned and set down another body below the first.

"There was another one?" Ariela gasped as he was still crouched over it.

"Two more. A woman and another man who was probably a hired guard," he explained as he straightened up.

"What happened here?" she whispered, more to express disbelief than ask an actual question, but her companion took it to be the latter.

"They're dead. That's all you need to know," he snapped, then left again, presumably to fetch the other body. She uttered a quick prayer asking for strength and patience, then finished her work and moved on to check his handiwork on the second body, only to find all was as it needed to be.

"That does it. Let's go," the warrior concluded after setting the third victim at the feet of the second.

"No, we aren't finished," Ariela argued.

"That's the best we can do for now. We don't have a shovel to dig graves nor are there enough stones around here to cover them. Let's go!" he insisted with a tone that said he would tolerate no more discussion. She hated to do it, but she had to trust him, so she stood up, brushed the dirt from the front of her dress, then picked up her bag and followed him as he set a rapid pace away from the carnage.

"Someone else will come upon them later and finish what we started. A legion patrol if nothing else," he assured her, then both were silent as they continued on their journey.

Chapter Thirteen
Bandit King

"This town belongs to me now!" Tallio shouted with his right hand held high while the left held the reins of his brown charger. He'd ridden up to the outskirts of Pralacus Templum with over fifty of his bandits to make his claim, and upon hearing him, townspeople in their homes for their noonday meal rushed to windows and doors to see what was happening.

The bandit leader swung his arm down, his men shouted in unison, then swarmed past him into the town with the mountains rising behind it. Women and children fled screaming back into the buildings while men grabbed axes and pitchforks and rushed to meet the charge while Tallio sat there laughing.

Not one bandit fell to the defenders as they easily knocked aside their makeshift weapons before stabbing, bludgeoning, or slicing them to death. A few of the younger ones dropped their implements and tried to run, but the bandit archers shot them down at a quick hand signal from Tallio.

"Soldiers!" someone shouted, killing Tallio's mirth. He watched as eight soldiers jogged up to the main street, each one wearing a steel breastplate and helmet, leather cingulum, plus leather bracers and greaves. They were equipped with a tower shield covered in brown canvas, a sword at the hip, and spear in hand. Upon reaching the middle of the street, they circled together and formed a phalanx when the first of the attackers charged at them.

"No, you fools!" Tallio screamed at them, but he was too late to stop the first of his men from being impaled.

"The rest of you pull back! Archers!"

Those who hadn't yet reached the phalanx slid to a stop in the dirt, then scrambled backward as the archers ran into range and loosed a volley. It did no good, as the arrows only bounced off helmets or embedded in shields.

"Up!" the enemy commander ordered from the center of the phalanx. The soldiers remained in their circle and rose as one, then marched toward the bandits in the town, most of whom backpedaled away from them, but of course there were two or three who were stupid enough to get killed attempting to break the shield wall.

"Archers, loose!"

He gave the order hoping something would get through now that the soldiers were slightly exposed, but they halted and locked down again before the arrows could hit.

"Pull back!" Tallio finally commanded as he glanced around for anything that could get through those shields.

All of his men were smart enough to obey this time and ran from the town. The soldiers broke formation long enough to chase them to the edge, but pursued no further and came back together in a single line to form a shield wall as the bandits gathered around Tallio.

"What do we do now, boss?" a black-bearded man in desperate need of a wash gasped between breaths.

"The best thing you can do is hold your tongue," Tallio snapped.

If only those soldiers would come out here to get them, then he could pick them off out in the open, but they just crouched there staring at him as he sat atop his horse and fumed.

The only advantage he had over them was numbers, but that seemed to be of little good against their training and equipment. But if that was all he had, he would find a way to make it work.

"All of you with shields, to the front," he growled, and nearly half of his remaining men stepped up to form a line in front of him. Their shields were a mix of circular and square designs, meaning they couldn't form a proper wall, but it was better than nothing.

"Two lines."

They bumbled around as they figured out which of them would move back, causing Tallio to roll his eyes as he resisted the urge to kill them himself. Their incompetence on full display for the enemy was embarrassing, but at least it might cause the defenders to grow overconfident.

When they were finally finished, the second line stood directly behind the ones in front of them, so he barked at them to stagger the lines to fill the gaps. Then he had the rest of the men do the same thing two more lines behind them, and at last they were ready.

"Archers, loose at will! The rest of you, charge!"

The half-dozen archers released one shot after the other as the footmen let out a fresh war cry and surged forward, somehow managing not to trip over each other.

None of the arrows did any damage, but they kept the soldiers pinned down. When the formation got close, the archers stopped launching arrows out of fear of hitting their own people. This allowed the defenders enough space to rear up and throw their spears, after which they drew their swords and put the flat of the blades on top of the shields.

Yet not even the disciplined soldiers could hold against so many crashing into them at once and the bandits barreled through their shield wall, knocking a few to the ground and scattering the rest.

Even surrounded and facing up to ten men alone, each soldier valiantly fought on, cutting down a couple more of the attackers but ultimately succumbing to the onslaught.

With no one to stop them now, the bandits swarmed into the town to kick down doors then drag out women kicking and screaming as well as bawling children. These people they left in the dirt as they set about ransacking homes and businesses, and a respectable pile of loot sat in front of every door by the time Tallio sauntered in, grinning.

He looked toward the ornate temple beside the lake to the north of the town where a half-dozen priests in their greenish robes stood within the colonnade, watching the events unfold. His men had yet to go near it, so he turned his horse with a tug of the reins and ambled up to look down at the priests with a wicked smile.

"How is the goddess today?" he taunted.

"She's happier when her worshippers aren't being slaughtered," a priest with a short white beard in the middle replied.

"Strange that she chose not to do anything about it," Tallio remarked, eliciting a mix of gasps and snickers from the bandits who had followed him.

"She will act when she sees fit."

"Which is likely never. She might incur the wrath of a god with some actual power."

This time, none of the bandits reacted while the priests glared at their leader, who continued to smile down at them.

"Boss, two of the soldiers are still alive," someone interrupted and Tallio looked left to see a middle-aged man wearing only the bottom half of a tunic looking up at him.

"Bring them to me," the bandit leader commanded, then he spurred his horse around and continued to the town forum. His men cast a nervous glance at the temple looming over them before hurrying back into the town, and he chose not to comment on their fear.

Upon reaching the forum, he rode up on the stage, keeping his horse's right flank to the kneeling crowd surrounded by his bandits, and looked down at the crying women and children, the few remaining young men making pathetic attempts to comfort them. Only the old men who hadn't taken part in the fighting dared to stare at him with any air of defiance, while the older women simply stared at the dirt.

"My name is Tallio Atroni, and I am your new governor. You will serve me now. The senate no longer holds power here," he revealed.

"You will burn for this!" a voice shouted from outside the crowd, followed up by a cry of pain.

The bandit leader followed the sound to see half a dozen of his men dragging a pair of armored soldiers toward him.

"I don't think so," Tallio responded with a wry smile as they finished their approach and his men threw them into the dirt before the stage.

"The army will destroy you!" the older of the two men, an enlisted officer by the rank of tesoro, declared, earning him a slap to the back of the head from the bandit to his left, the helmet ringing from the blow. The bandit then held his hand with the other and clenched his jaw as his face turned bright red.

Tallio rolled his eyes at the simpleton, then to the tesoro he remarked, "They haven't managed it yet. What have I to fear from them?"

The tesoro didn't speak in favor of glaring at him with naked hatred.

"What are you going to do with us?" the other soldier asked, and Tallio leaned back to address the entire crowd.

"People of Pralacus Templum! You will be allowed to live your lives as before. All that is changed is you will now be sending your goods to me instead of the senate."

"Tell that to those you killed!" one old man spat.

"How many did the Naerans kill to conquer this land?" Tallio responded with a pointed look.

He waited several seconds, but no one dared argue with that logic. So he turned his attention back to the soldiers to decree their fate.

"As for you, I am ready to let you live. In return, you will train my men."

"Why would we do that?" the tesoro demanded to know, angry and defiant while his companion looked far less sure of himself.

"You would get to live, and you will be paid and provided for the same as any of my men."

This gave the man something to consider, and he finally chose to be silent.

"Take these two somewhere they can think things over," he ordered those guarding the prisoners, then to the crowd he said, "As for the rest of you, go back to your business. See to the dead and wounded, repair any damage, and do not attempt to leave."

Coarse laughter drifted down the road from people yet to come into sight, the volume of mirth exceeding even that of the water rushing against the pylons of the dock upon which Fasius stood. There could be no doubt who was coming, so the wiry old man dropped his torch into the bin of straw and resin-covered pine wood which soon spewed black smoke into the clear afternoon sky, signaling his sons on the other side of the river to ready themselves.

A gang of bandits appeared up the road, which was little more than a dirt path, and he patiently waited as they approached while swapping stories of their recent successes and guffawing all the while.

Chief among these stories was their takeover of the nearest town a few hours earlier, something which Fasius had already learned from a teenage boy fleeing the slaughter. He had been the only one to make it this far, having been returning from fishing the river nearer the town when he saw the bandits ransacking the town and wisely ran for his life.

Although he'd previously granted passage on his ferry to these criminals, Fasius knew this was going to change how they treated him and sent his sons to the other dock with the boy and a plan while he stayed here to deal with the bandits who couldn't be far behind.

"What's with the fire, Ferryman?" a muscular young man called out as they drew close. He bore the look of an athlete, possibly a wrestler grown bored of the sport and looking for new challenges.

Two of the five were in mismatched leather armor with no helmets, one only wore a dirty tunic with a belt, and the last two were in nothing but a dark leather kilt which was the garb commonly worn by Esberan peasants, their darker skin confirming them to be natives of that land. All had their weapons out, the Esberans with gently curving swords while two of the Naerans carried axes and the last one a wood club.

"The old codger must be cold," the tunic bandit piped up, and they all snickered as the sweat shone on their exposed skin. Fasius stayed quiet, leaving it to them to make the first move.

"We now control this whole area, including your ferry," one of the armored men revealed, now that they were done with their jokes.

"I heard," Fasius responded quietly.

"Good. Then you won't be surprised to hear we will no longer be paying for passage."

"Yes, you will."

"Pardon?" the athlete, apparently the group's leader, questioned as he took a menacing step forward.

"I cannot operate for free. My family and I would starve."

"There's nothing stopping you from charging everyone else."

"No one else is going to be coming this way anymore."

"Look old man, if you want to live, you will do as we say," the leader threatened as he took another step forward, coming close enough for Fasius to smell the stench of his breath.

"Kill me, and there will be no ferry. Look," he explained, then took a step to the side and held out his hand toward the other dock where his sons were just within sight across the wide river. Two held torches above stacks of sticks and dry grass, one beside the raft and the other by the tiny dock house. The third stood below the guide rope with an ax poised in both hands.

"They won't do it," the bandit reasoned.

"If you hurt me, they'll destroy everything and run to the city. Then you'll have no other way to cross except the southern bridge, which is at least two days from here."

The group leader backed up and began chewing on his left cheek as he looked from the ferry master to his sons and back again.

"I will discount my services in exchange for protection, but that is the best I can do," Fasius offered before the man hurt himself trying to figure it out on his own.

The bandit looked at his men, but all they did was shrug or shake their heads.

"Fine, but don't expect any favors," he finally growled before stomping away with his men following.

The ferry master took a deep breath as he watched them go, then turned to the river and waved his arm several times in a wide arc until he saw his sons back away from their positions and begin readying the raft to come get him.

After organizing a defense of his town, which included patrols in the immediate area, Tallio had gone to the roof of the stablemaster's house and now stood staring toward Naera. Soon, that city and all the lands it claimed would be his and he would be their king.

But why stop there? he thought as he glanced toward the snow-capped mountains in the east. Those fools in the senate could have so much more, but were blind to their own power. Once he was in charge, he would lead his people to victory over the Esberans and beyond. He would be more than a king. He was set to be an emperor!

"It is good to see that the training we gave you is proving useful, when you actually decide to use it, that is," the observer commented after stepping up beside him.

"I got the job done."

"It could have been done with fewer losses."

"Then maybe you should train these fools as well," Tallio challenged.

"Who is the greater fool, the one who leads, or the one who follows?"

The bandit leader, or king as he was coming to think of himself, whirled on his guest and held up a finger to his face as he growled his next response.

"Watch your tongue or I'll cut it out."

"Do not presume to threaten me, Savage. You know all too well that my people wield power beyond your understanding and that I could incinerate you on the spot if I wish," the observer shot back in a rare display of emotion.

Every muscle in Tallio's body tensed as he fought to think of a comeback, but his mind locked on the image of that extraordinary city and his thoughts froze from the overwhelming number of wonders he had witnessed.

He could try to deny it all he wanted, but not only did he need their help to overthrow the Naerans, they could destroy him any time they wanted. Their choosing to support him when he came to them with nothing while running from the law was a puzzle he'd long since given up trying to solve.

Finally turning away from the taller man, he repeated his question.

"Why haven't you trained my men?"

"Our instructors are needed at home, and we will not expose ourselves by bringing people to us. At least now it seems you've solved the problem on your own, proving you to be a worthy ally, even if you are a bit slow."

The bandit ground his teeth together as he chose not to dignify that with a response.

"Your progress is such that we are ready to provide you with additional aid," the observer continued a moment later.

"What more could I possibly need from you?"

"This town is not defensible. You need a fortified fallback position to protect yourselves and your resources. We can help you with that."

"How?"

"Our engineers can design a fort and we will even loan you workers to build it. Our methods can have it finished within a month."

The bandit king smiled wide as an image of a palatial fortress formed in his mind.

"I accept your offer," he agreed as he headed to the stairs.

"Where are you going?"

"To find the perfect location."

Chapter Fourteen

The Return

"I never imagined so many people living in one place and building such structures!" Ariela marveled as they passed through Naera's western gate and entered a bustling marketplace.

"It is how soft people stay alive in a hard world," Raldus responded sullenly as he set a quick pace toward the city center. A passing man in a bright white tunic and yellow sash looking to be in his thirties overhead the comment and paused with clear intent to rebut it, but a single glare from the armored warrior sent him scurrying on his way..

Having learned to recognize when Raldus didn't want to speak, and wouldn't, Ariela said nothing more and silently beheld these wonders.

Multiple rows of merchant stalls stretched out of sight to the north and south, and people of many skin tones and body builds wandered among them. The calls of vendors promising quality merchandise at incredible prices rose above the dull roar of conversation from the crowd. She sensed a certain reservation in the voices and movements of both merchants and patrons, challenging how she imagined such a busy place would look and feel.

The shoppers rushed from one stall to the next, speaking as little as possible, and the merchants offered few luxury goods and instead competed to sell various food items. Preserved items such as the salted fish from Kostrai were among the most popular.

Raldus gave the scene an unsettled look as they passed, which told her he also noticed something was out of the ordinary, but she did not request an explanation.

Nearly all that noise dissipated within seconds of exiting the marketplace to be replaced with an air of solemnity as people walked in and out of massive buildings fronted by towering white columns gleaming in the summer sun. Men in robes, the bright colors of which varied from one building to the next, stood at the entrances beneath vibrant banners bearing strange symbols and/or depicting people.

"The temples of the gods," Raldus remarked without prompting.

"There's so many of them," Ariela gasped in disbelief, and Raldus nodded twice, his manner suggesting he found the whole thing to be a bit ridiculous. Was that also how he thought of her and the beliefs of her people?

As they walked past the temples, the sound of flowing water grew in volume until they came to a set of stairs leading up to a giant circular platform supported by arches to span a river. Ariela didn't even notice when she slowed to gaze upon the boats floating gracefully atop the clear water, many of them moored to the docks along the banks while a few sailed past.

The platform blocked her view when she neared the bottom of the stairs, and she looked up to see Raldus already at the top watching her with an impatient gaze but restraining himself from scolding her. Her face grew warm upon realizing her childish actions, and she used both hands to hike up her skirt to free her feet to jog up the white stone steps, keeping her eyes down as she ascended.

She quickly forgot her embarrassment when new wonders revealed themselves upon looking up again. The platform turned out to be the city's main plaza and it was ringed by shrines, some of which sported the same symbology as the temples they'd just passed, but there were also many that she didn't recognize. A large stage broke this ring at each of the cardinal directions, in front of which were dozens of people listening to criers shouting the latest news.

"Bandit raids continue across the countryside! Senate urges citizens to avoid travel unless absolutely necessary!"

"Increased Navy patrols on Inno Speigudel have halted tribal raids in Republic lands! Attacks on hunting parties continue over the border!"

"The Eagle Legion is now laying siege to the Esberan city of Yishapur!"

"Senate debating harsher punishments for a wide range of crimes!"

Most of these names and places were unknown to her, but the announcements still gave Ariela a clearer picture of how bad things were and how the Naerans were struggling to hold things together. Her heart went out to all these people, and she grew dizzy trying to think of how she could help.

All of this also told her it was only a matter of time before one of these conflicts reached her home, and that her own people's survival lay in the hands of those whom they'd feared for so long.

Raldus led her to the center of the plaza, where there was an enormous bronze statue of a muscular, bearded man in a toga holding a globe above his head. Around this statue was a gray brick wall around three feet in height topped by short, tapered capstones, while on the stones between the statue and wall was a mural depicting scenes of nature along with symbols which she did not recognize. There was one opening in the wall on the east side, next to which stood a priest in a sky-blue robe and dark green sash, while on the ground beside him were a few pairs of sandals.

"Wait here. It is perfectly safe, and I won't be long," Raldus instructed, then left his bag on the ground and walked off without awaiting a response. She watched him head to the nearest stage, but became distracted when a couple not much older than her approached the priest, bowed their heads to him as he gave a blessing, then removed their sandals before passing through the opening.

"Do you wish to enter the shrine?" the priest asked Ariela.

"Why did they remove their shoes?" she questioned instead of answering.

"The stones honor Livaria. Worshippers must remove their footwear in respect."

"Who does the statue represent?"

"You do not know Keslu?" the priest asked with his head cocked to one side. There was no hint he had taken offense, but she still felt her face grow warm once again and she glanced down before shaking her head.

"He is god of the sky, and Livaria is his wife, goddess of the earth. Their love protects us from evil," he explained, then added, "Your clothes are strange. From whence do you come?"

"A community in the great forest," she responded, careful not to give away too much. Fortunately, he did not press the matter.

"Did they not teach you of these two?"

Her response was two quick shakes of her head.

"Then enter. Study the mural and the writings upon the statue base. Learn of them."

"My god forbids this," she refused.

"Ah, you serve a jealous god. Now I understand."

Her head shot up as she nearly exclaimed that there was only one God, but then she remembered it was not her place to instruct a man, so she pressed her lips together and looked back down, but not before catching his pretentious smile.

"It is alright, Child. You need not fear him. I will tell you how you can be free of him."

"I *am* free!" she blurted out before she could stop herself.

"Then enter the shrine and satisfy your curiosity."

Oh Raldus, where are you?

She considered walking away, not out of any fear she might give in or any consequences for doing so, but rather that she doubted she could control herself for much longer. However, there was always the chance that Raldus would have trouble finding her, even on the other side of the shrine given its large size, plus she wasn't sure she could carry his bag as well as her own.

A few worshippers entered and exited as she stood there staring at the bricks and the priest left her alone, presumably to give her time to work up the courage to defy her god.

"You need to enter and learn the truth," he sternly commanded after several minutes had passed.

"That is not why we are here, and you have no more authority on what is true than her or myself," Raldus' voice interjected, and she looked up at him, making no attempt to conceal her relief.

"You dare disrespect me!" the priest exclaimed as he fixed his gaze upon the warrior. The increase in his volume drew the attention of others nearby, including the couple from before as they were exiting, but now they halted in the opening and earnestly whispered to each other.

"If I choose to disrespect you, there will be no doubt to what I would dare do," Raldus stood his ground, causing a flurry of whispers among the onlookers.

The priest stepped forward as if to strike him, but Raldus did not flinch as he spoke before the man could take a second step.

"You can't leave your position until your relief arrives, unless you intend to forsake your vows."

The priest glared at him, but stepped back and seethed in place.

"Let's go," Raldus directed Ariela as he grabbed his bag before turning and strolling through the crowd without missing a beat. It was all she could do to pick up her own sack and hurry after him.

"I'm sorry for causing trouble," she apologized after catching up.

"Don't be. These priests like to act superior to everyone else, and someone has to stand up to them now and then."

"Do our monks also act like that?" she asked, wondering if she was somehow blind to it.

He didn't answer at first, long enough for her to fear she'd crossed a line, so she chose not to press the issue. They reached the stairs at the north end of the plaza and descended to a wide street with few people around and relatively plain buildings on each side.

"Your monks have their arrogant moments like most people, but on the whole, they treat everyone as an equal, including an outsider such as myself. They also seek more knowledge and do not presume they already have all the answers," he finally told her. Apparently, he just needed time to think out his response.

That made her feel better about things, and she started looking around again with renewed desire to take in all she could of this amazing place.

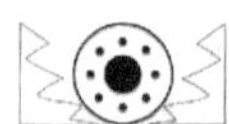

He dreaded seeing the other warriors again, but his desire to get started on his mission outweighed the discomfort, so Raldus turned off the street into an alley that should get him to the army offices a little quicker.

"Where are we going?" Ariela asked.

"Either no one at the plaza knows where the warriors are assembled, or they're too afraid to speak to me. We're going somewhere I'm sure to find answers."

"Why would they be afraid?"

Her questions were a little annoying, but also helpful in a way. They kept him from dwelling too much on the past and its implications for the upcoming reunion, adding to her presence in keeping him grounded.

He was about to answer the latest one when two people blocked the other end of the alley and began walking towards them, the light behind them obscuring their features. He put a hand on Ariela's shoulder to stop her, then used it to turn her with him to go back the way they'd come, only to discover two more shadowy figures blocking that direction.

Acting on instinct, he shoved the woman into a doorway while also dropping his bag, then drew his sword and pressed his back against the opposite wall where he could see her and all four strangers.

An all too familiar laugh rose in response to his actions and continued until the four men closed the distance, staying far enough back to not initiate combat.

"Amili?" Raldus wondered aloud as he lowered his guard a little.

"Most of us thought you were dead," the owner of the laugh announced, his voice confirming it was Raldus' old classmate. Now that they were closer, he could see that all of them were wearing the leather armor favored by most Stoneforge warriors for its ease of use when traveling.

"Why would you think that? I won all our duels, and you're still alive," Raldus taunted.

"Maybe someone got tired enough of your arrogant mouth to murder you in your sleep. However it happened, we figured it could be the only reason you weren't already neck deep in this fight."

Ariela stirred as if to step out into the alley, but stopped when Raldus signaled her to stay by showing her his left palm. The others looked at her as if noticing her for the first time - a rookie mistake if it were true - and Amili put his hand on his sword in preparation to draw.

"So, you're enslaving little girls now, are you?"

"That's vile!" Raldus countered, spitting at the other man's feet.

"The code does forbid such things, but you never really cared about the code, did you?"

Raldus returned to full guard, both hands on sword and holding it up at his center, and three of the warriors drew their blades while the fourth made a move to grab Ariela, who at this point was crouched down with one hand digging around in her sack.

"No!" Raldus shouted. The opponent on his right stabbed at his midsection, but he blocked the move by sweeping his sword around and pinning the other's against the wall, then held it with his right hand to free his left long enough to drive his elbow into Amili's face.

A short scream drew his attention to Ariela, who was using both hands to slap at those of the man reaching for her while trying to scoot further back into the doorway and grunting from the effort.

The one warrior yanked his sword free from under Raldus' who forced him back with a kick to the midsection, turning just in time to block an overhead strike from Amili on his left while the remaining aggressor struggled to join the combat in the tight space.

"What is going on here?" a deep voice roared from the right. All five warriors instantly disengaged and stood at attention in place while a large brute of a man stomped down the alley toward them. Ariela used the distraction to move her pack in front of her to hide behind in the corner she'd squeezed into - a few quiet sobs the only sign of any distress.

"Elder! We found this man leading a girl down this alley and we're trying to free her!" Amili stammered, conveniently failing to mention Raldus' name.

No one said anything more as the older man finished striding up to them. He approached Raldus first and got in his face, revealing his own to have skin darkened and stretched from many years in the sun and brown eyes hardened by witnessing unspeakable things.

It took him only a second to recognize the young man, and he backed away with a snort and a scowl.

"Form up!"

The four warriors organized into two offset lines in front of the elder with Ariela's doorway between him and them. Raldus went to join them, but the elder shoved him back against the wall.

"Is there not enough fighting for you right now that you have to attack one of our own?"

"He's been gone for a long time and he's never respected the code, sir," Amili protested. The elder closed within a few inches of the young man and spoke in a low tone that clearly made him fear for his life.

"The code rules all of us, including him. His only mistake is to test its boundaries, but he has never violated them."

The elder glared at his subordinate for a long time to ensure he'd made his point, then finally dismissed the four of them, who turned and hurried away as he scowled at their backs.

"I apologize for their behavior, ma'am. My name is Elder Proclus," the older warrior told Ariela in a kindly tone after they were out of sight. He held out his right hand to help her up, but she hesitated and looked at Raldus, who nodded to her as he sheathed his sword, after which she accepted the hand and pushed aside her bag.

"Are you hurt?" Raldus asked her as he stepped close and looked her up and down.

"No, he barely touched me. Are you?"

"They've never been able to touch me," he bragged.

"What about your injuries?" she inquired further as she reached toward his sides, but he stopped her by gently grabbing one of her wrists.

"I'm fine," he insisted through clenched teeth. In truth, there was a sharp pain growing in both sides, but he wasn't about to admit it, especially not in front of an elder.

She looked up into his eyes, her own hazel ones still misty from the fright but full of determination. Clearly she meant to insist on making sure he hadn't undone any of the healing from the past few months, but something in his expression got her to change her mind as she nodded instead, covering anything she was thinking or feeling by checking on the bags.

"I'm surprised to hear you speak well of me," Raldus confessed to Proclus, who had watched the exchange with his normal stern expression but tinged with something the young man couldn't quite identify.

"Don't think too much of it. You have honor, but you're also an imbecile," Proclus countered.

The remark reminded Raldus of home, but the memory evoked little emotion. Ariela had finished checking the bags and already lifted hers to a shoulder, so since he had nothing to say, he crouched down enough to grab his sack and toss it over his shoulder. It took all his discipline to resist wincing from the soreness, but he managed it and swept his free hand forward palm up to indicate for Proclus to lead the way.

"What happened to you, Raldus? Amili is also a fool, but he's right about you being gone for too long. What could keep you so busy that you almost miss this nation's worst crisis since the first Esberan war?" the elder inquired after they'd exited the alley and were back on a road.

"I was injured on a job and have been recovering at a town in the great forest," Raldus replied, being in no mood to give details.

"Are you saying you lost a fight?"

He didn't respond at all, by speech or gesture, and just kept walking.

"Answer me, boy."

Nothing.

"What do you know about it, girl?" Proclus turned his attention to Ariela, who was staying on Raldus' right side.

"Leave her alone," Raldus hissed.

"I *might* let you get away with not answering me, but don't *dare* to give me orders!" the elder threatened him, then repeated his question to Ariela.

"He hasn't spoken of it," she responded softly.

"Is my father here?" Raldus asked, attempting to change the subject.

"No, he is with some veterans in the north dealing with the tribes while most of the army handles things in Esbera," Proclus answered after casting a scowl at the young man beside him.

"How could everything get so bad in a matter of mere months?"

"Nobody knows for certain, but the best anyone can guess is that this bandit, Tallio Atroni, has been getting help from somewhere. He has more food and equipment than he should, and his tactics are worthy of an army officer, but they insist he's never served the republic. The Esberans are the prime suspect, but there's no chance they could be consistently supplying him so much over the mountains."

"Where did he get so many men?"

"Most of them come from within the republic itself; desperate men with no other way to feed their families, greedy men seeking riches, and dumb boys trying to look tough. The rest are the usual crooks from Kostrai and Esbera."

"I find it hard to believe so many would choose to follow him and risk facing the army."

"His reputation drew them in, especially when they started telling a story of how they managed to kill a Stoneforge Warrior," Proclus explained with a pointed look to his side, but Raldus did not take the bait.

They arrived at the city garrison then, a large complex where the soldiers protecting and patrolling the society were housed and trained, sparing him from any further attempts at drawing out his story.

The elder warrior instructed the clerk to find a bunk for Raldus, then told Ariela to follow him to her accommodations. She had hoped to get her companion alone long enough to insist on checking his condition after that fight, but when she looked at him for support, he just told her she was perfectly safe and to go with Proclus. Knowing better than to argue with him in front of others, she complied and followed the middle-aged man back into the street.

"Tell me how you came to know him," Proclus commanded once they were underway.

"I don't think he wants me to do that," she resisted as she kept her eyes fixed on the ground. This elicited a long, frustrated sigh from the man that showed he was on the verge of losing his patience.

"Is it customary to respect your elders where you come from?"

"Yes, of course."

"This holds doubly true for warriors who must trust the teachings of their elders to get them through a fight alive. I chose to let him save face, but I will know all I can about what happened."

"Is it really that important?" she asked, then looked to the side when he shot her a surprised look.

"You're awfully curious for a woman," he stated, his tone stern but not holding any anger. She also noticed that this was the first time he called her woman instead of girl.

"I don't want him to be angry with me," she replied meekly.

He gazed at her for a long time, even as they continued walking, seeming to study her as if she had suddenly become an opponent of a variety he'd never before faced.

"He knows that I will keep asking until someone answers me and won't be angry that you told me so he doesn't have to, at least for now. He's never lost a fight in his entire life, and if he has now, it could affect him in battle," he finally explained as he looked ahead again.

That sounded reasonable enough, and she saw no reason to mistrust this man's intentions.

"He was beaten, and we think his attackers believed he was either already dead or would be soon, but he managed to crawl through the forest before fainting right outside our town. It seemed sure that he would die, but I was asked to tend to his injuries anyway. He spent the next three days delirious with fever, but then it broke and he began to recover."

"You were responsible for his care?" Proclus questioned in surprise, and she nodded in confirmation.

He suddenly stopped and grabbed a passing soldier by the collar of his armor and pulled him up to face him.

"Take this woman's bag to the inn housing the nurses," he ordered as he took her bag from her and shoved it at the young man.

"I'm not on duty," the soldier protested.

"Does it look like I care?" Proclus challenged. The soldier started to argue again, but stopped himself, donned the helmet he'd been carrying under his left arm, then accepted the bag and trudged off.

"Thank you," Ariela called after him, but he didn't react.

"I'm going to take you to the hospital. A lot of people are getting hurt in this fighting and it sounds like you can do a lot to help them."

Chapter Fifteen

The Face of the Enemy

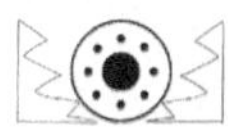

Upon nearing Pralacus Templum, the town taken over by the bandits two weeks prior, Tesoro Cassius had split his scouting group into five pairs and sent each one in a different direction. Two were to go around the town perimeter to see what they could without being spotted themselves; meanwhile, the other two made a wider circle to look for outlying camps between the river and mountains. The tesoro chose Raldus to go with him, one of the other warriors went wide with a soldier, and the last warrior stayed behind to watch their rally point.

Dark clouds shrouded the afternoon sky, but they did not yet threaten rain and the gloom would aid them in their task.

It was slow going as the enemy had actually set up patrols and sentries for which they either had to wait until they passed or sneak around them. Fortunately, it wasn't at all difficult given that the bored men were more interested in drinking and talking than paying attention to the world around them.

"You've fought these cretins before, correct?" the tesoro whispered after halting atop a hill with the town in sight below them. To reduce the risk of being seen or heard, everyone in their party was wearing dark leather armor with helmets and one sword, which for now remained in the scabbard on their left hip.

"Yes."

"Anything you can tell me about them?"

"They win their fights with numbers. One of them alone is nothing to fear."

The tesoro nodded, then signaled Raldus to follow with a wave and started down the hill in a slight crouch.

"I didn't expect them to be this organized," Cassius remarked when yet another sentry, this time on a rooftop, blocked their approach.

"They've gotten better since I saw them last," Raldus admitted.

"Better work our way around the outside," Cassius suggested, and Raldus nodded his agreement.

Having approached from the southwest, they slowly made their way north with both of them keeping watch for anyone who might discover them and looking for an opening into the town.

That opening did not appear, and they found themselves on the north side working their way east.

"This is new," the tesoro observed when they came upon a wide, dirt road leading from the town toward the mountains northeast of them.

"It's a solid design," Raldus mused as he gazed upon the ditch and the raised dirt surface. The visible ruts despite its recent construction indicated it was well-traveled, but it was holding strong.

Movement several paces to the other side of the road caught the warrior's eye, and he pointed it out to the tesoro. It turned out to be the other pair of scouts, so Cassius signaled them to follow the road on their side before indicating for Raldus to follow him with a jerk of his head.

They followed along beside the road, passing beside the lake for which the town was named but not crossing the river, until nearly a mile later it went further into the mountains between two steep slopes. An empty cart bouncing down the street sent them into hiding once, but that proved to be the only traffic they encountered.

When they reached the mountainside, they hid behind an old rockfall, and the tesoro proceeded to study the road and the opposite slope with a deepening frown.

The sounds of metal tools striking rocks echoed down from further up the road, indicating either mining or construction, but the source remained well out of sight.

A long sigh passed the tesoro's lips as he made his decision, and he caught the attention of the other team long enough to signal them to fall back.

"We should see where this goes and what they're doing," Raldus protested in a hoarse whisper.

"There isn't enough cover, and too many places for them to have sentries we can't see. It's too much of a risk."

"It does no good to go back without fresh information. We've barely learned anything here!"

"It does even less good for us to get killed and not report anything at all. Now move out!" Cassius hissed. The warrior ground his teeth together in frustration, but obeyed and followed to return the way they had come.

They were the first to reach the rally point as the sun dipped below the clouds to turn everything a shade of orange, and the warrior watchman declared it to be all clear. While they waited for the others to arrive, Raldus looked to the north while studying in his mind all he had seen.

He would find a way to learn what they needed to know.

Since most of the fighting was so far away, Ariela spent most of her time in the ward caring for those fleeing their homes or small towns in the countryside and coming to the city for protection. Many of them were weak from hunger as they didn't have enough time to gather supplies before leaving their homes, while others had suffered sprains or broken bones from accidents on their journey. Some were also hurt from fighting amongst themselves over rations or for no other reason than the flare-up of a bad temper, a fact which wearied her almost as much as the constant work.

These people fighting among themselves made no sense to her. They were all in the same situation, so why couldn't everyone just work together to make the best of it and help each other?

When she started thinking this way, she reminded herself of all they had gone through and drove off the growing resentment with compassion. The blood ran hot in times of trouble, causing anyone to lash out for little reason, so she reminded herself of this fact and focused on helping and not judging.

The stories she heard them tell were terrible, of houses burned when the residents refused to cooperate to entire groups slaughtered on the road for what little treasures they possessed. Nearly all of the young men were on either side of this conflict, leaving their wives, mothers, and/or children to fend for themselves. The women stayed strong for the most part, but the children were much harder to help with their persistent questions for which she had no answer.

"How are you doing?" a familiar voice asked from behind her as she was tucking a feverish woman into a cot. She looked over her shoulder long enough to confirm it was Raldus, still in his leather armor and smelling of sweat and grime, indicating he'd only now returned to the city from whatever he'd been doing these last weeks.

"I'm getting by," she answered, then looked back at her patient long enough to ensure she was comfortable. A quick nod confirmed that she was, so Ariela gave her a comforting smile as she held the woman's cheek with her left hand, then she straightened up and turned to give Raldus her full attention.

"People are treating you well?" he asked.

"Yes, they have been most kind to me. How are you?"

"I'm fine," he grunted as he averted his eyes and looked out over the ward set up in an old warehouse by the river. Sunlight streamed through a few high windows while over a dozen lanterns attempted to drive away the remaining shadows, and the bells of the boats added an almost soothing ambience to counter the groans of the patients.

"No fresh injuries?" she double-checked.

"No."

"Any pain in your ribs?"

"No," he answered again, but this time she could tell he was lying. Not only did broken ribs take a long time to completely heal, she'd also gotten to know him well-enough to understand his body language. It was imperceptible to most, but at that last question he had stiffened up while once again averting his gaze.

"Come over here and I'll check to be sure," she prompted, then stepped around him.

"I need to get back to work," he asserted, heading toward the door.

"Do we have to argue every time!" she declared to his back, her voice rising. He stopped and turned just enough to give her an annoyed look, and her face grew warm as she realized her tone had caught the attention of others nearby.

"I don't need looking after," he growled at her.

"No, but isn't it best to know for sure you are ready to fight?" she questioned meekly, still embarrassed but refusing to give up.

He glared at her while she avoided his gaze by staring at his chest, then he sighed and came back to her, at which point she led him over to the wall where there was a wooden crate under a window.

"Why do you keep doing this?" he asked after sitting down and she'd started unbuckling his armor.

"I want to make sure you are well," she responded, not sure of his meaning.

"Why?"

She looked into his eyes and saw he was looking at her with a sense of wonder that held more than simple curiosity about her wanting to help him.

"You know it is our way to help anyone in need," she deflected upon returning her focus to the armor straps.

"You have gone far beyond that."

She chose not to respond as she finally finished removing the armor and placed it on the floor next to them.

When she looked up, she couldn't help but catch his eyes again and saw he was still watching her with the same look, but she just continued with her work and he didn't press the issue.

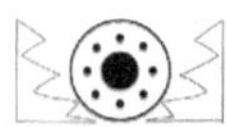

His identity safely hidden by the stolen leather armor, filthy tunic, and dirt-smeared face under a steel helmet, Raldus strolled into Pralacus Templum with nothing but an exchange of grunts between him and the road sentries. A light rain fell, but everyone ignored it as each drop brought a welcome coolness from the otherwise hot day.

It had been a week since the scouting mission, but this time he came on his own so he could be free to actually accomplish something.

He made his way to the town forum where he discovered two soldiers standing before a group of at least twenty bandits shouting instructions, their steel armor and demeanor revealing their nature. Despite clearly being there to train the bandits, neither one bore a weapon and two pairs of bandits in complete sets of heavy armor and holding weapons stood on each side of them.

These must be soldiers garrisoned in the town and taken prisoner upon its capture. The armor and training seemed to indicate they had agreed to work with, or for, the bandits, but the guards suggested that their new employers didn't trust them.

Whatever the case may be, there was nothing he could do about it, so he continued on to the north end of town. At least this explained the recent increase in the abilities of the bandits to organize a defense screen.

"Where do ya think yer goin'?" one guard beside the new road leading to the mountains challenged.

"To take a leak, whassit to ya?" Raldus shot back.

"Ya know ya nee' Tallio's say before goin' to the fort."

"An' I thought I join to do what I want."

"Is there a problem?" a familiar voice questioned from behind, and Raldus stiffened as he turned to look at the new arrival. It was indeed the same man who oversaw his defeat in the great forest, and he even still carried the warrior's sword at his hip.

"Someone jes' a bit los', is all," the guard explained with a slight quiver in his voice.

The bandit leader peered at Raldus, who stared back as he imagined how it would feel to impale the creep here and now, but he held back. He could kill the man before someone stopped him, but would certainly be dead himself shortly afterward.

"Get out of here!" Tallio sneered, causing him to nearly draw his sword at the tone, but then he forced himself to nod and hurry away.

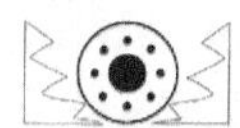

The two armored guards wearing dark green capes and green-plumed helmets each held up a hand to stop Raldus as he approached the meeting room. The one on his right closely checked his Stoneforge tattoo, then nodded and let him pass. By all accounts, he shouldn't be here, but the soldiers were used to the warriors doing their own thing and trusted them implicitly. Fools might suggest they were too scared to try to stop him, but anyone with sense knew the consequences for a guard failing in his duty were far worse than anything a warrior would do to him.

"These 'mere bandits' have seized a town and are building their own fort nearby, and they've already thwarted several attempts to drive them out!" a man exclaimed as Raldus entered the room.

No one present seemed to notice his arrival except for Elder Proclus, who glanced up from the circular table next to which he was standing, then looked back at the others gathered around without reacting.

The room turned out to be more spacious than he would expect for its simple purpose, with the large open windows opposite the door making it feel even more so. A gentle breeze blew through those windows, cooling the space and fluttering the banners on the walls, each one the same dark green color with four wavy blue lines in the center. This was the flag of the republic with the green representing the natural bounty of their land and the blue lines symbolizing the waters of life where their ancestors built the city.

"These are not bandits any more, if they ever were. Start calling them what they are - rebels," a short, but fit, man declared. He wore a breastplate of overlapping steel segments with a dark green cape affixed to the shoulders. The armor was a new design of which Raldus had only heard, but not yet seen. That, and the helmet with the light blue plume on the table in front of the man identified him as a tribune of the army.

This mix of soldiers, warriors, and politicians was still trying to decide what to do with the information he'd brought back from his scouting missions. For over a month now, they had done nothing but gather tidbits of information and secure supply stores. When were they actually going to get something worthwhile accomplished?

One of the first things he did upon returning each time was to check on Ariela. She'd taken right to her nursing duties, her gentle soul bringing comfort to the sick and injured while their bodies healed under her care. The others had accepted her as one of their own and saw to it she had everything she needed and was as safe as anyone could be in these circumstances.

Despite being kept busy in the ward, she still made time to check on him when he came by. He tried to stop her the first time, but she pressured him into allowing her to examine him and he finally gave up resisting. He hadn't sustained any fresh injuries yet, and he hardly felt any remaining pain from his old ones, but she insisted she needed to keep an eye on them to make sure they weren't regressing.

That was why she'd come along after all, right?

He wasn't so sure anymore about that being her reason or his for allowing it. She'd exceeded his expectations and adapted to her new world without any trouble, and he was beginning to wonder at the immense depths of her soul.

"Bandits, rebels, it doesn't matter what we call them! They must be destroyed!" a tall, pudgy man in a sky blue toga and purple sash shot back, snapping his thoughts back to the moment.

"That's what we are working on, Senator," Proclus growled with his jaw clenched.

"The problem is that our cavalry and siege engines are all in Esbera," the tribune interjected.

"Can't you put some soldiers on horses and build new catapults?"

A disbelieving glare was all Proclus could manage in response to that, and Raldus suspected his own expression matched. The tribune took a deep breath in an obvious attempt to maintain his patience before replying.

"It takes months to properly train a cavalry unit. Regular soldiers can't just hop on a horse and do the same job."

"Our warriors are trained horsemen, but are too few and too valuable to risk without additional army units," Proclus added. The tribune shot him an offended look, but then seemed to consider it and gave a brief nod, accepting the fact that a warrior trained since childhood was of more value than a conscript trained for mere months before being deployed.

"What about the catapults?"

"Under construction, but the rebels will likely attack again and capture more territory before they're finished."

"Unacceptable!" the senator roared as he slammed a fist on the table, nearly causing Raldus to laugh at how little the table and the objects upon it moved from the impact.

"I will kill their leader. Without him, the rest will go home," Raldus finally spoke up.

The senator and tribune looked over at him in surprise, clearly noticing him for the first time, while Proclus just watched him with a stony gaze.

"Who are you?" the senator questioned.

"One of our warriors," Proclus answered in his stead.

"Can he do as he says?" the tribune asked.

"Probably."

"What makes you so sure the rest won't keep going?" the senator pressed.

"I've faced this man once before. His ego is what drives him. Men like that make sure that those around them rely on them for everything."

"You're awfully young to know such things about men."

"The nature of men is part of our training," Proclus revealed. The elder warrior watched his junior with a concerned frown which departed from the attitude of the man Raldus knew from his youth.

"Even if they don't disperse, the loss of a leader will make them vulnerable, especially if he hasn't selected a successor," the tribune chimed in, his voice quiet and thoughtful.

"What do you need to get this done?" the senator inquired.

"Nothing from you," Raldus responded as he looked at the man in his blue eyes above his flabby cheeks. Despite the warrior's harsh tone, the senator appeared pleased about this while the tribune looked relieved, but Proclus' face furrowed even more as he tiredly leaned on the table with both hands and locked eyes with Raldus.

"You'll die if you do this."

"You said he'd succeed!" the senator objected.

"In killing the renegade leader, not in surviving the job."

"The others would attack him in the heat of the moment, even if they do end up deciding to give up afterward," the tribune explained.

"I will kill him and end this madness," Raldus insisted.

"You can't do this alone," Proclus asserted.

"It's his choice," the tribune rationalized.

"No. We will go much further combining his skills with our numbers and resources."

"This is my fight!" Raldus announced as he advanced on the table.

"There's that selfish arrogance I've always known, and here I was ready to believe you had finally become a man," Proclus challenged without changing position.

Raldus could only glare at him in response, but the senator had taken a couple steps back and was now fearfully looking from one to the other while the tribune watched with an expression that could be either amusement or pretentiousness.

"I finish what I begin. This is my fight," Raldus declared.

"It's everyone's fight now, even that girl's. Are you going to get her killed too?"

This prompted Raldus to fling the nearest chair to the floor as he took off around the table at his elder who reflexively stood up and braced himself for the assault, but a soldier standing guard jumped in front of the young warrior and pushed him back with his tower shield.

"That's enough!" the tribune bellowed before Raldus could recover. When he did, he stood there staring at the soldier, who returned his glare of murderous intent with a gaze of quiet determination.

"Perhaps..." the senator started, but the tribune cut him off.

"The elder is right. Any real chance for success requires a coordinated effort, even if all we do is rout them after the deed is done."

Raldus glared at the soldier a moment longer, then cast a scowl at Proclus before returning to his previous position across the table, and the guard returned to his post after receiving an affirming nod from the tribune.

"This is your idea. Do you have any suggestions for making it work?" the senator proposed in a trembling tone as he slowly stepped back up to the table.

All were silent as Raldus grit his teeth in thought. The expressions of the senator and tribune were of simple expectation while Proclus looked ready to say something sarcastic.

"Divide the legion into smaller groups and attack the town in multiple waves from various angles. Include two or three warriors with each one, and have another group of only warriors. Take the town, then seize the fort."

"We'll get slaughtered without cavalry to protect our flanks," the tribune refuted.

"They'll be expecting you to send in the entire legion in a single brute force attack. Going in smaller waves will catch them off-guard."

"They still have archers, which means the only way to get close is to use a shield cover march, and that will give them more than enough time to organize a counterattack."

"Then we move quicker," Proclus interjected. His expression had changed from imminent sarcasm to quiet reflection with his eyes cast downward at the map laid out on the table.

"What do you mean?" the senator questioned, attempting to stay relevant.

"Everyone carries as little as possible. Leather armor, smaller shields, and no spears. We run in and destroy them before they even know what's happening."

"Shock and awe," the tribune inferred.

"Exactly."

"It could work, but we don't have enough of those types of armor or shields to equip an entire legion."

"We use whatever armor we can find, even linen will be enough for this, and we can make new shields far quicker than any siege equipment."

"And in the meantime, we can harass the enemy with smaller attacks to slow them down and prevent them from moving on before we're ready," Raldus added.

Everyone looked around to see if anyone had anything else to say, but no one spoke up.

"Get started. I'll inform the senate and let you know our official decision by the end of the day," the senator agreed, then left the room.

"I'll brief my officers and start preparations. You do the same with your people," the tribune remarked as he donned the helmet before also leaving the room.

"There's hope for you yet," Elder Proclus told Raldus with a slight smile, and a warm feeling of pride rose within him at the compliment, despite still wanting to say something nasty.

Chapter Sixteen

The Gathering Storm

The group of eight Stoneforge warriors near the city's east gate looked at Raldus as he crossed the large stone brick plaza. The fountains gushed clear water and bronze statues honoring past heroes shone in the sun as people of all kinds went in and out of the taverns, inns, and shops around the square. Most of the waiting warriors had their arms crossed or hands balled into fists, while the rest just watched him with quiet resignation.

All were equipped with the standard fare of their order: dark brown leather cuirasses with the Stoneforge crest in silver on the right breast, belts with leather strips all around and spatha sword hanging from the left hip, sandals with straps wrapping around the calves and leather greaves in front, and finally a leather bracer on each wrist. A stiff leather case containing a small bow was slung to their left shoulder to hang on their back, and a small linen sack rested at their feet.

"What do you mean he's in charge? He hasn't been one of us for three years, and never did *any* jobs for the town!" one of them, a stocky individual by the name of Markus, protested. Elder Proclus responded by getting in the man's face, forcing him to look at him instead of Raldus.

"He has never stopped being one of us, and his job experience is not up for debate," he hissed as Raldus took up position behind him to the right.

"But, Elder..."

"Silence! You will do as *I* command."

A sort of staring contest ensued, during which Raldus looked over the warriors assigned to him. They'd all trained together, but he noticed that each of them was at least one year his junior, which made sense given that anyone older or even matching him in age would likely never obey his command, no matter what anyone else said.

Since speed and stealth was required here, Raldus had elected to leave behind the steel armor gifted to him by the monks and was instead attired the same as the others.

Markus finally broke eye contact with the elder and averted his gaze down and to the left in a minimal show of respect and obedience. Proclus gave a sharp nod to signal his approval, then stepped back to stand beside Raldus.

"Childhood rivalries have no place here. No one knows how to survive better than a man who has been without support for many years, and Raldus knows the enemy. He is your best chance to inflict considerable harm and come back alive."

The elder looked them over with an expression which dared them to object. They didn't look any happier about the situation, but no one offered any new complaints.

Satisfied for now, Proclus turned away from them and leaned toward Raldus to whisper so quietly that even he struggled to make out what he said.

"Don't screw this up. Remember that others have skills that complement your own."

Having said his piece, he stalked off without waiting for a response.

"Let's go," Raldus prompted in a stern voice, then resettled the bag on his right shoulder and marched off through the gate.

"What are we?" Vibi asked his friend as three Pralacus men loaded a supply cart with shovels and pickaxes in front of them.

"Bandits," Titus responded.

"And what do we do?"

"We rob people."

"So let's go rob someone!"

"Huh?"

The loaders finished, and the lead bandit watching them nodded his approval. Vibi sighed as the driver whipped the mule and pulled away, the wheels creaking under the weight.

"When was the last time we actually robbed anyone?" he continued.

"I dunno."

"Exactly. They brought us here to train with those soldiers, then we got stuck here. From what I hear, hardly any of us go on raids anymore. We're all stuck guarding this town or building that fort."

"Boss says we need it."

"Why?"

"I dunno," Titus repeated, prompting another sigh from Vibi.

"It feels like we've become something else, and I have a feeling it's going to get us all killed."

"You worry too much."

This time Vibi chose not to respond and instead stared off into the distance.

He'd come here looking for adventure, something better than the dreary grind of town life. When the army came to his home looking for new conscripts, he had fled so he could live his own life without all those rules and other people bossing him around. Life as a bandit was great at first with them spread out in isolated camps and basically doing as they pleased, but now things were pretty much how he'd always imagined life in the army.

All of that was bad enough, but there was an increasingly tight feeling in his chest and stomach at the thought that this couldn't last forever. The republic may be spread thin right now, but it was still powerful, and it must only be a matter of time before they destroyed Tallio and all who followed him.

Perhaps it would be for the best if he went his own way again?

Except there was always the chance Tallio would win, and there would be no hiding from him. Anyone who defied him now would be at the top of his list of people to die in some grand spectacle.

Were his only choices to die at the hands of the army or the boss?

The fresh legion of reservists stood outside the eastern gate looking resplendent in their armor, which shone in the morning sun, adding a sense of awe to the occasion as the people lining the sides of the road stood in solemn silence. Tribune Herius studied the near one-thousand troops from atop his white stallion, his own segmented armor not nearly as bright as the solid pieces worn by his men. However, the sky-blue cape billowing out behind him added an air of nobility which boosted the aura of authority granted him by the helmet with the plume of matching color.

Satisfied with the appearance of the troops, the tribune looked up to the top of the gate where he could see the consul flanked by four of his consularians in their dark armor with midnight-blue capes and helmet plumes. When their eyes met, the leader of their people raised his right hand in a simple benediction, and Herius turned his horse with a tug of the reins.

"Ready! March!" he commanded.

"Forward, march!" his prime confirmed.

The drummers set the pace with two single strikes followed by three in quick succession, the tribune spurred his horse, and the entire column moved forward, the ground trembling with each step.

"Prime Darius! Lead the chant! The People's March!"

"Yes, sir! Men, ready?"

"Ready!" the column responded as one.

They continued steadily forward as Darius shouted each prompt with the soldiers repeating it, the history of their people swelling their hearts with pride and boldening them for the fight ahead.

Long ago, evil did come.
Long ago, evil did come.

The old gods turned away.
The old gods turned away.

Our people were set a'wandering.
Our people were set a'wandering.

Many years in foreign lands.
Many years in foreign lands.

Their spirit they did keep.
Their spirit they did keep.

A new evil sought to seal their fate.
A new evil sought to seal their fate.

In a desert at the end of the world.
In a desert at the end of the world.

Into the treacherous mountains, they did flee.
Into the treacherous mountains, they did flee.

Scattered, lost, and afraid they were.
Scattered, lost, and afraid they were.

Their end did not come.
Their end did not come.

Ways through, they did find.
Ways through, they did find.

Into paradise, they emerged.
Into paradise, they emerged.

A new life they did create.
A new life they did create.

The wilds they did tame.
The wilds they did tame.

Peace was theirs at last.
Peace was theirs at last.

Evil did learn of them.
Evil did learn of them.

And came for them once again.
And came for them once again.

Great strength it did find.
Great strength it did find.

The people stood together.
The people stood together.

Favored by new gods.
Favored by new gods.

They defeated all enemies.
They defeated all enemies.

Now it falls to us.
Now it falls to us.

To defend home and people.
To defend home and people.

All who dare threaten us.
All who dare threaten us.

Shall feel our wrath.
Shall feel our wrath.

And soon will be no more.
And soon will be no more.

Naera! Naera!
Naera! Naera!

For thee, we march!
For thee, we march!

Death we will face.
Death we will face.

So you may live on.
So you may live on.

Honor our names.
Honor our names.

And we shall wait for you.
And we shall wait for you.

In the land of eternal light.
In the land of eternal light.

Naera! Naera!
Naera! Naera!

For thee, we march!
For thee, we march!

Naera!
Naera!

March!
March!

For the republic!
For the republic!

All cheered together, and Tribune Herius led them away from their great city, caring not who saw him smiling proudly. They would put down these criminals and all their people could get back to living and working - secure in the knowledge they were safe from all harm.

"Not even the Naerans with all their boasting have ever built anything this fast," Tallio remarked as he watched the workers below him. With just a little over two weeks of work, the fort was already taking shape at the mountain's base, positioned between two ridges that extended towards the gorge facing his town to the south.

A gray, stone wall with a large gate at its center now marked the western perimeter, the first structure to go up. Its smooth face blended seamlessly with the ridges at each side, looking as though it had always been a part of them despite the careful geometry revealing its man-made nature.

"This is only a glimpse of what we can do," the observer remarked from his right.

The bandit king rolled his eyes, then went back to watching the workers scurrying about like ants on the lower part of the slope behind the wall. It was only three days since they finished the wall, but already they'd flattened areas for the first buildings and were now hard at work laying the foundations. The cleared dirt and stone were separated into piles of various sizes next to each building site, and lines of men carted the debris in wooden barrows to a mixing station at the center of the complex.

His benefactors made such progress possible by sending a team of engineers and laborers to manage the process. Their clothes were Naeran, but there was no disguising their bronze skin or strange accent, which prompted whispers among the bandits. None had questioned who they were as of yet, and the whispers quickly disappeared when Tallio came near, so at least the men knew their place.

"Boss!" someone shouted. He snapped to alert and looked to the gate in time to see a young man wearing a brown tunic and riding a ragged mare trotting up the slope toward him.

"What?" he yelled back, recognizing the man as one of his scouts, ignoring the subsequent annoyed sigh from the observer.

The man rapidly finished his approach and pulled up on the reins to bring his horse to a sudden halt before the two of them.

"A legion has camped beside the west bank of the Oeculous Fluvio and destroyed the ferry!" the scout gasped.

Any pleasure Tallio had been feeling over the fort's progress evaporated as heat surged through his body and he clenched his hands into fists.

"They destroyed the ferry?" he verified, growling the words through clenched teeth, and the scout nodded as he continued catching his breath.

"It was always a matter of time before they struck back, but this is of no consequence," the observer interjected.

"We can't get across the river."

"Neither can they, and when this fort is finished, you will be in control of all the land between the river and the mountains."

"They will attack us soon."

"It will take time for them to bring more troops across the southern bridge and up to meet us. The fort will be ready by then, you will destroy that expedition, and you will be free to send your own forces back across the river to harass the enemy at your leisure," the observer assured him.

"There are still two forts, a city, and Stoneforge on this side. The latest from Esbera says the legions are winning, so they could return soon, bringing Esberan auxiliaries with them."

"The outcome of that war is not yet certain, and it will be a long time before it is decided either way. We will give you what you need to lay siege to the forts and cities, including troops, but we can only commit those resources once you establish a foothold."

"And Stoneforge? They can't be sieged."

"I have sent word to my people of the threat they pose, and they will find a way to remove it," the observer guaranteed.

What he was saying made sense, but Tallio still didn't like it. The Naerans were no fools when it came to warfare, and he had a feeling they were planning something yet to be revealed. It was a small comfort that any attack had to come across the river since the legions from the nearby forts were deployed across the borders. Their remaining garrisons weren't enough to threaten him, and would be kept close to protect their positions.

Life was much simpler when all he did was steal stuff and hide. Now, a part of him was wondering if the power was worth all he had to do to get and keep it.

"You!" Tallio declared, pointing a finger at the scout whose breathing had finally steadied. "Find yourself a fresh horse and get back to the river. Watch their every move and send word if they do anything. Take someone with you."

The scout hurriedly nodded, then spurred his horse, galloped down the hill, and through the gate to get to Pralacus where they still had the majority of their resources.

"You!" Tallio repeated as he pointed to another bandit standing nearby, a young man in leather armor holding a spear who pointed to himself to confirm it was indeed him to which his leader was referring.

"Yes, you! Organize a small party of scouts and send them south. I want to know when anything comes our way. Also, get messengers to our camps across the river."

The bandit nodded his understanding, then picked up his spear and trotted down the hill.

"Perhaps it's time to set up a chain of command," the observer mused.

“Don’t tell me what to do,” Tallio grumbled as he ambled down the hill. He’d better go to the town himself and make sure those two didn’t mess things up.

A flickering orange light showed in the deep darkness ahead, prompting the group of warriors to draw their swords and stretch out to either side of Raldus with up to six feet between them. These seven crept forward, conscious of every footfall on the grassy ground, while the remaining two stayed behind to watch their backs, bows out with arrows nocked.

This was the first time he’d led anyone, whether into a fight or otherwise, but he trusted them to know their business, so all that was required of him was to indicate what he wanted and leave the details to them.

A slight movement not far ahead caught Raldus’ attention, and he threw up his left hand to signal the others to stop. As he focused on the spot in question, the shadowy shape of a man slowly formed in the darkness.

Camp guard.

The warrior watched long enough to ensure that the man hadn’t detected them, but the slight movements of his head showed that he was alert. There was no way any of them could get close enough without being seen or heard, and even switching to a bow to shoot him might be enough movement to give them away.

Making his decision, Raldus looked over at the warrior on his left who immediately looked back, then repeated the action with the one on his right. Once he had their attention, he signaled for a charge on his command, and they confirmed their understanding with a single nod. The others would know to follow them in.

When they were ready, he lifted his left fist where they could both see it, held up one finger, then a second, followed by a third after which he flattened the hand and swung it forward three times and broke into a run on the last one.

They charged without uttering a sound, but there was no disguising their movement or silencing their footfalls at this pace. The guard had just enough time to call out a single shout and grab his sword by the hilt before Raldus was upon him, grabbing the side of his head to slam his face into a nearby tree as the others rushed past him.

Four bandits crawled out of their one-man tents with swords in hand, but the warriors easily dispatched them before they could get to their feet. Raldus jogged up to join the others, noticing a shadow on either side darting into the woods, which indicated the other guards were fleeing. No one bothered to give chase.

"Finish off that first one and tell the rest of our men to join us," Raldus ordered one man, who nodded before walking off, his pace quick but unhurried.

His next orders were for four of the men to take up watch, one on each side, while the rest of them searched the camp for anything important. Those who checked the evenly spaced four tents ripped the canvas from the poles to check inside, then tossed the fabric into the stone ringed campfire to create more light by which to search the sacks lying around the camp.

"I bet you think you didn't even need us for that," Markus muttered as he searched.

"It would have taken longer. This was quicker, and that has its benefits," Raldus concluded as he tore open a sack in which he found only a few lumps of bread.

"What, you're not going to brag about how much better than the rest of us you are?"

The warrior he'd sent away returned with the two who had guarded their rear. They glanced at Raldus and Markus, then busied themselves with the search.

"No," was all Raldus bothered to say.

"Go on. You know you want to."

Raldus threw the bundle of rags he was holding into the fire, sending sparks into the air as he stomped up to Markus, who rose to stare back at him. The others kept busy as a pretense of not listening.

"What do you want from me? An apology?"

"That would be a start."

"Tough. I am a better fighter than you and the others. Get over it."

"There's the Raldus we know, cocky as ever. What makes you so much better than everyone else, huh?" Markus taunted, his voice rising as they both ceased to care about any remaining bandits in the area.

"Beating you and everyone else every time we sparred and getting the highest marks in every training course doesn't speak for itself?"

"We all got the same training, and we all received warrior status!"

"That doesn't make us equals."

"We're not good enough, so you decided to strike out on your own."

"How else was I going to find a real challenge?"

This remark elicited a small chuckle from the other man as he stepped up to Raldus, causing him to have to look up into the taller man's face. Differences in height aside, each was clearly as fit and strong as the other.

"What makes you a better person than me, or them?" Markus intoned, cocking his head to indicate the others with the last word. Raldus didn't respond at first and merely looked into the other man's accusing blue eyes.

"I said I was a better fighter, not a better person," he clarified. Markus stepped back, confusion swiftly overtaking his features as he stammered to respond.

"Is there anything of value?" Raldus asked the others without taking his eyes off his verbal sparring partner. They'd been standing there awkwardly for a few minutes now.

"Nothing," one of them answered.

"Then let's get out of here."

"This was one of our camps?" Raldus asked. Their search for outlying bandit posts had taken them to the site of a previous skirmish, where all that now remained was a few tent poles with tattered cloths flapping lazily in the breeze. They'd entered with swords drawn, but it was clear no one had been here in weeks, so they sheathed them to take a look around.

"Yes. They managed to kill everyone. We're still not sure how," Markus exposited. He'd been rather quiet the last three days, ever since their confrontation after routing the enemy patrol.

"What's this?" Raldus questioned as he stooped over a stone at the edge of the camp and ran his fingers over a black streak on its side.

"Scorch mark," Markus revealed after walking up to get a look at it. Raldus rolled his eyes, but was careful not to let the other see it, and reined in his sarcasm before responding.

"I can see that, but what could cause this pattern?"

"A gust of wind fanning the flame of a fire, perhaps?"

"Possible, but the campfire was over there," Raldus argued with a tilt of his head toward the ring of stones several feet to his right, then he stood up to search for any other marks but stopped when he saw the fear in the other man's eyes. Not a fear of him, but of something else.

"What aren't you telling me?"

He looked around at the others, each one bearing a similar expression, then back at Markus, who opened and closed his mouth more than once without speaking as he sought the right words.

"We recovered the bodies a few days after the attack. There were many of them that we don't know what killed them."

"How can that be? Did they not have any wounds?"

"They had wounds, but...," Markus started before trailing off as if uncertain what to say.

"They were unlike anything anyone has ever seen before," one of the others chimed in.

"Explain," Raldus demanded. Markus and the last one who'd spoken glanced at each other, and the former took a deep breath to steady himself.

"Something burned right through their armor and flesh. We thought flaming arrows at first, but there were no puncture marks, only burns, and none of this was on those who had arrows still in them."

"Could it have been another type of flaming weapon, such as a sword?"

"We don't think so. There's the lack of cuts on the bodies, but when we first arrived, there were also more marks like that one all over the place. They've just been covered by the grass or dirt by now."

"That would seem to indicate a ranged weapon which missed a few times," Raldus puzzled out, to which the others nodded in response.

"But no such weapon exists!" a warrior blurted.

"Not that we know of," another remarked.

"Even if it does exist, how did a bunch of bandits get their hands on it?" Markus posited.

"Perhaps that's the answer right there," Raldus interrupted, causing all of them to stare at him wide-eyed.

"What is that?"

"They could have staged all of this to make us think they have some powerful new weapon. Poisoned anyone who surrendered, then used heated metal rods to create the wounds and markings."

The others fell silent as they considered this new possibility, but they all looked rather unconvinced. It didn't sound all that likely to him either, since even if these crooks were smart enough to think of such a thing, it didn't actually do enough damage, to morale or otherwise, to be worth all that effort.

"Whatever it is, weapon or clever ruse, we'll figure out how to deal with it. Come. It's time to rendezvous with the others," he finally concluded and confidently marched out of the camp.

The wood creaked and groaned as the sails billowed from a fresh morning breeze to aid the rowers as they sailed upstream on the Oeculous Fluvio; the river named for the first consul of the Naeran Republic.

"It's going to be another warm day," Prime Arius remarked as he looked up at the brightening sky, his left hand on his hip beside the sword and under his segmented armor. He could feel the weight of his helmet and its green-plume from the leather chin strap digging into his skin, but as uncomfortable a sensation as it could be, it was one to which he had long ago grown accustomed.

"Yes, but the days are growing shorter. Let's hope we can finish this business before they start cooling as well," Centurion Trevin remarked as he monitored the activity of the men, his own armor immaculate and matching that of his superior except for the plume running from side to side instead of front to back.

"You worry too much," Arius teased as he looked back down at the deck where the half-naked men were working hard to trim and align the sails to get the most out of the wind in the fight against the current. Neither officer had to order them to do this, and the prime's heart swelled with pride at seeing the noble discipline of his crew.

"Which reminds me, how is the army going to get troops across the river with the bridge taken out so we could pass? I doubt they're going to put it back just to have to take it out again a few weeks from now when this is all over," Trevin wondered aloud.

"I'm sure they'll lay some sturdy boards over the gap for now."

The prime looked behind them to the south as he thought of the massive stone bridge near the city of Asturios, now with a sizable gap in the middle. The bridge was large enough to span the river and allow easy travel between the city and the rest of the territory. However, it was not tall enough for a war galley to sail beneath, so laborers from the city had needed to dismantle it in part.

One of the many inconveniences of war.

That problem was behind them for now, and the prime turned his gaze to the north toward the next one.

"We should reach the camp by midday, and the legion will be across the river in less than a month. These rebels will not survive even a week after that."

This time Trevin only nodded, his eyes never wavering from his observing every movement of the sailors.

"Enemy ho!" the call came from the crow's nest, and both officers glanced up to see where the lookout was pointing, then followed the finger to the east bank where a pair of leather-clad men on horses were watching them from beside a stand of trees, partially hidden by the leaves of some bushes.

"Archers!" Arius shouted, and a team of six bowmen rushed to the starboard rail and took aim. Seeing this, the rebel scouts spurred their horses and turned to run, but it was too late.

"Loose!" Trevin ordered, and bowstrings twanged from the release. The volley of arrows arced up from the ship, then sped down toward the hapless scouts. One struck its target in the back of the neck, knocking him forward off his horse, while two more hit the horse of his companion behind the rider.

The horse cried out in pain and reared up, throwing its rider to the ground before returning to all four hooves and galloping away. There was but a moment where the rider remained motionless on the ground, but then he scrambled to his feet and stumbled away as fast as he could.

"Out of range," Arius grumbled as the man ran for his life.

"Now they will know we're here," Trevin remarked.

"No matter. There's nothing they can do about it."

Trevin nodded his agreement, annoyed that they failed to stop the scout from reporting in but only feeling a wounded pride, not any worry about what the rebels could do with the knowledge of their presence.

The scout ran out of their sight, so the two of them sighed and returned to their place in front of the helm.

"Back to work!" Trevin barked at the men who had stopped to watch, and they hastened to look busy.

Chapter Seventeen

We Are Coming For You

"Is this supposed to worry me?" Tallio asked of the whelp struggling to catch his breath before him. The barefoot boy had burst into his office at the highest point of the fort and blurted out a scout report as if announcing the end of the world.

The office, made of quarried stone, was rather appealing with its open west-facing doorway and centrally located windows in the other walls for sunlight. There was a bed with a feather mattress beneath the eastern window, while a stolen table and chair with gold trim sat by the southern window, allowing a view of the stairs.

He'd always imagined living like this one day, but so far was finding it a strange feeling after having lived nearly his whole life outdoors with nothing but a tent for shelter if he was lucky.

These were the thoughts the boy had interrupted, leaving him in no mood to deal with the wide-eyed preteen still staring at him.

"They're destroying our patrols!" the runner cried.

"Get out of here!" Tallio roared as he shoved the boy out the door.

"Excellent leadership strategy, as always," the observer commented from his position beside Tallio's desk. He'd almost forgotten the pest was there, doing nothing as usual.

"Don't you have anything better to do?" Tallio accused as he stomped to his chair and plopped into it.

"Not at the moment. Why did you treat that boy in such a manner?"

"I don't have to explain myself to you."

"Why are you angry? You have more power now than you dreamed possible a year ago, and it continues to grow. I would think this would be a joyous time for you."

"The republic isn't defeated yet, and I'm not angry. I'm just tired of having to explain myself every five minutes, especially to brats barely old enough to hold a weapon."

"Your people need to believe in you. Perhaps it would be wise to dispatch a fresh patrol to eliminate those conducting these attacks."

"Waste of time. We're safe here, and any losses are easily replaced. When we move out, we do so in force," Tallio grumbled as he picked up a quill and began scribbling on the parchment on the desk before him. Record-keeping, yet another nuisance that came with his growing influence.

The observer watched him for a while, not saying anything but also not leaving. He was obviously considering saying something else, but the bandit king wasn't interested in hearing it.

Minutes ticked by as he pretended to work, and he was considering getting up and throwing the man out, the consequences be damned, but then someone else stumbled into the room. Upon looking up, he saw one of his scouts in scratched leather armor, torn tunic, and bruised face.

"Boss," the scout gasped before collapsing to his hands and knees. The observer was next to him, but all he did was look down at the man with thinly veiled disdain as Tallio jumped up and went to him.

"What is it?" he asked after kneeling in front of the man.

"A galley - on the - river."

"What, coming upstream? Towards us?"

The scout nodded as he fought to steady his breathing, and Tallio slowly stood as he processed this information. Random attacks on his patrols he could ignore, but this was a far more serious development.

"Why is this significant?" the observer questioned.

"The nearest naval fort is near Izagion in the north at Lake Speigudel, and the Oeculous Fluvio doesn't connect to it. It takes a long time to send a boat down the Nurvita Fluvio to connect with the Oeculous and come back up this way," Tallio said quietly, both as a means of answering the question and thinking through the issue for himself.

Before any of them spoke again, the sound of a galloping horse, then the loud neighing of it being pulled to an abrupt stop, drew their attention outside. Tallio looked out the window in time to see one of the scouts he'd sent to keep watch on the legion camp jumping off the animal then jogging up the stairs, and he resisted the urge to groan as he waited to hear whatever news this one carried.

"They're..." the new arrival started to say as charged in, but then he tripped over the other one still on his hands and knees in front of the door, which sent both of them sprawling to the floor.

"Wretch!" Tallio shouted at the newcomer as he reached down and helped up the injured man. He then told the first scout to go get some food and rest as the other one scrambled to his feet while stammering out profuse apologies.

When the first one had left, the bandit king turned to the one who had barged in, his face now bright red, and bade him speak.

"A bridge. They're building a bridge."

"Who is?"

"The legion camped by the river. They're building a new bridge across it."

"Get out," Tallio growled, and the scout obeyed as quickly as his shaky legs could carry him.

"They mean to attack here," the observer commented.

"Clearly. They brought the galley to protect the builders."

They were both silent as Tallio stared at the floor, his sour mood forgotten while he figured out what to do.

"I cannot solve this problem for you," the observer declared with a tap of his staff on the floor.

“I didn’t ask,” Tallio retorted as he glanced at the staff. Its power could destroy that boat and probably the bridge as well, but they dare not risk backing the republic into a corner, scaring them into raising even more troops to use against them. The only thing stopping the garrison at Fort Tryit in the south from attacking was the senate order to protect the road in case an Esberan expedition came through the mountains.

No, he would have to do this himself.

Somehow.

“You stay here and finish the fort. I’ll deal with this,” he finally asserted as he stomped out.

Small circles of flickering orange came into sight ahead in the early morning mist, and Tallio held up a hand in a signal for the men behind him to go even slower. They then crept forward as silently as possible until the shadowy shapes of tents formed in the retreating darkness, at which point he stopped and crouched down with his men following suit. The sound of the gently flowing water to their left worked with the quiet and the morning chill to create a sense of peace that did nothing to ease the roiling in his gut.

He had crossed the river with two dozen men using boats taken from local fishermen, then had joined up with ten more from one of his camps on this side. A team of ten archers he’d sent down the east bank to await his signal before attacking the galley.

It wasn’t enough to rout the legion from its camp, but all they had to do was burn that bridge so he would have enough time to prepare his own defenses and eventual counterattack.

Squinting into the mist, Tallio looked for a path to the bridge, using his memory to fill in what he couldn’t see, and also checked for any signs of danger. There was one sentry by the river and three more spaced about ten feet apart in a line, a torch burning behind each one.

Behind the sentries stood a rough picket fence of both upright and angled stakes. The bandits couldn't see it from this angle, but Tallio knew there was also a ditch in front of the fence, as was common practice.

No way to sneak into the camp for a surprise attack, but the soldiers would wake soon, so the time to strike was now.

Tallio looked behind him at the archer he'd brought along, the cloaked man nodded, then nocked an arrow and held it down for the boy next to him. The boy struck his dagger on a piece of flint to send sparks flying over the arrowhead wrapped with an oil-soaked cloth.

"Who goes there?" a sentry called out when the arrow caught fire.

"Now!" Tallio shouted and charged forward. His men followed, but the archer hung back long enough to send up the signal.

Tallio knocked aside the spear of the first sentry, then plowed his right shoulder into the man's chest, knocking him to the ground where he plunged his sword into the armor opening right below the man's neck as his men rushed past him.

One of the other sentries blew a horn before they could get to him, and the clear ringing of the galley's alarm bell drifted over to them.

"To the bridge! Burn it!" Tallio shouted as the camp burst to life. Soldiers rushed up with weapons in hand as officers burst out from their tents to bark orders at their men.

One of the other sentries charged Tallio with spearpoint down before he could follow his men, but the bandit king juked to his left, grabbed the spear with his left hand, and pulled back. When the sentry fell forward, he struck him in the back of the head with the pommel of his sword to send him crashing to the ground. His helmet likely prevented any serious injury, but the blow was still enough to stun him.

Now he was free to go after that bridge with his men, so he ran after them, but when he saw them seconds later, he slid to a stop, almost falling backward from the sudden change in motion.

Heavily armored soldiers surrounded all his men, walling them in with their shields, and they were now moving to the center of their circle, stabbing the bandits as they went. He watched in disbelief, going unnoticed as the soldiers kept slaughtering the attackers one by one even when they tried to surrender.

He looked over at the half-finished bridge, so close yet so far, then beyond it to the galley raining down arrows on the east bank, with none coming from the other direction.

With one last look at his men, he turned and ran away, grabbing the archer by the shoulder and pulling him along when he got to him.

The fight that morning was over within minutes, but over two hours later, Ariela still felt somewhat rattled. They had been so close, and all she could do was sit in her tent and pray.

When it was over, she had gone straight to the hospital tent only to find there was nothing for her to do. One soldier was dead, but the few who were hurt had suffered nothing more than some minor cuts and bruises, and all the attackers were dead.

So now she stood on the burnt remnants of the ferry dock and watched the builders on the bridge, their machines driving support beams into the riverbed. Anything to keep from seeing the dead bandits get carted off to be burned.

"Are you well?" a gravelly voice asked kindly, and she looked left to see Elder Proclus had come up beside her. She wasn't surprised that she hadn't noticed, both due to his light step developed over years of training and experience and being consumed by her own musings.

"Why do they do it?" she questioned with a glance toward where the fighting had taken place, after which she quickly returned her gaze to the bridge.

“Greed, foolishness, revenge for some perceived misdeed,” Proclus answered as he took up position beside her to watch the construction as well.

“I don’t understand.”

The elder lightly sighed, then responded, “No one does. Poets and scholars pretend to, but they have rarely seen such things for themselves.”

“There must be a reason for them to want to hurt and kill others, and risk the same for themselves,” she persisted.

“Not everyone needs a reason,” he declared, and she felt a lump form in her throat at the thought.

“Why?” she choked out, more as an expression of despair than an actual question.

“Be glad you do not understand, child. If you did, you would probably be one of them,” Proclus concluded, then turned and walked away.

Her vision blurred with tears as she thought of all those affected by this violence. Families driven from their homes, children separated from their parents, and mothers who would never see their sons again.

In the end, that one word was all she could think about.

Why?

Chapter Eighteen

This Is Our Town

Upon hearing that Raldus' group was approaching the camp, Ariela asked to be excused from the work in the hospital tent and the lead nurse granted her permission as she looked at her with a warmly shrewd smile.

She arrived at the camp entrance as the warriors were walking past the wooden pole fence, their expressions tired but their movements strong as ever. It had taken a little less than a month for the army to make all the preparations for this fight, from equipping the soldiers with lighter armor to building a new wood bridge across the river. Raldus and his group of warriors had been out harassing the rebels this entire time.

When he saw her, Raldus dismissed his men, then approached her and held out his right hand in a signal for her to lead the way.

As she turned and walked toward an empty tent, she allowed herself a small smile at the fact he didn't bother to resist her checkups anymore.

Once inside the tent, he began removing his armor while she undid the ropes holding open the flaps. When they were closed, she helped him by taking the armor pieces and setting them on the table while at the same time watching his movements with occasional glances at his face. It seemed his stiffness was all but gone, and she didn't see him wince in pain even once.

Soon enough, he was standing there in nothing but sandals and loincloth, and she began probing his ribs for any sign of bruising.

"Are you in any pain?"

"Not for some time now."

There was a time she would have suspected him of lying, but had finally come to trust him to be honest with her. Besides, his flesh was firm to the touch and didn't recoil or quiver from the probing.

His ribs were the last of his injuries to heal, but to be on the safe side, she had him hold out each arm one at a time so she could check for any sign of reinjury. This also gave them more time together, although she wasn't sure either of them were ready to recognize why that should matter.

"Have you had any trouble using your sword?" she asked upon reaching his right wrist. She held the forearm with one hand and held the tips of his fingers with the other, moving the hand up and down to feel the flexibility of the wrist and listening for any popping or cracking sounds from what had been a particularly nasty break.

"No."

She didn't hear anything, and it flexed fine, so she let him put his arm down and moved on.

"It looks like you're healed and won't be needing me anymore," she concluded upon finishing, looking down at the dirt as she spoke.

"I haven't needed you for some time now," he stated without emotion, and she had to turn further aside to hide the sudden hurt threatening to burst out into tears. A part of her knew this to be the truth, and had known the entire time, but she had been reluctant to admit it out of the fear it was the only reason for any friendship between them.

He stepped up to her, cradled her chin in one hand, and raised her face to look up at him again.

"I have wanted you around, and still do," he confessed, and she did not try to hide the huge smile his words brought forth.

Suddenly looking fatigued, he let her go and turned to the table to don his tunic.

"What's wrong?"

He just kept gathering his things without responding, an all too familiar reaction from him, but she decided she would no longer let him get away with it.

She walked up behind him and set her hand on his back below the neck, which was enough to get him to stop what he was doing, but he still didn't look at her and simply stared at the inside of the tent.

"Did something happen out there?"

"Nothing important."

She thought about letting it go, but something told her she couldn't let him face this fight without first confronting whatever this was.

"I heard that the leader of these bandits is the same man who nearly killed you. Is that the problem?"

"No," he sighed, shrugging off her hand and turning away to leave her standing there awkwardly.

"I realize I know very little about the life you live, and I understand even less, but you should know by now that you are not alone," she tried to assure him.

No reaction.

Sighing, she walked past him, pulled open and tied back the tent flaps, then stood in the opening and turned back to him to say one last thing.

"Remember what you learned during your time with us. Your people believe in many gods that they are never sure actually hear their prayers, but mine place their faith in a single one whom we believe is the only one and are confident does look after us. He asks only that we trust him, and promises to be there when we call. It's time for you to make a decision."

She held his gaze for a few seconds, then whirled around and headed back to the hospital tent with her heart pounding in her chest. He hadn't reacted at all, but she still couldn't believe that she had dared to speak to him in such a manner, even going so far as to issue a command.

She only hoped that no matter how he felt about her attitude, he would consider her words and they would somehow help him deal with whatever was bothering him.

"It will be dawn soon," Tribune Herius remarked to his stoneforge colleague, who only nodded in response.

The two of them stood outside the command tent in the center of the camp on the western side of the river which flowed past Pralacus Templum further east. It was eerily quiet in the nearly empty camp under the starless sky as a cool breeze blew through the camp, a herald of the coming autumn. The hushed voices of the surgeons and the few women allowed to come and assist floated to them on the breeze and he dared not reflect upon the job they would soon be called to do.

"Are all your people in place?" Herius asked.

"We are ready when you are," Proclus assured him.

"Then it is time," he sighed, then nodded to a nearby archer and donned his helmet before climbing on his black horse as Proclus did the same.

The archer nocked an arrow with a strip of oil-soaked linen wrapped tightly around the head, held it up to the torch on his left to light it, then fired it into the air over the river.

They watched the fiery light as it arced across the sky while the horses snorted and stamped beneath them. The officers with their units already outside the town were no doubt issuing the first orders of battle upon seeing it.

When the arrow had fallen to the earth and out of sight, the well-groomed tribune and his grizzled companion nudged their horses into a gentle trot. Within seconds, they were out of the camp and crossing the bridge, the thuds of horse hooves on wood echoing louder than the splashing of the brown water against support posts beneath them.

This day would either mark the end of the rebel threat–or the beginning of many years of sorrow.

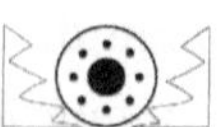

Shouts, screams, and the clashing of metal on metal rose from the town nearly a mile behind Raldus and his group. This made it difficult for them to wait where they hid in the rocky crag, and continue watching the dirt road leading up to the bandit fort, but they had their job and those at the town had theirs.

The bright sun drove away the morning chill upon its rising, and now Raldus' tunic was growing heavy with sweat, his impatience from his desire to get into the fight serving to increase the flow. For this battle, he wore the steel armor given to him by the monks instead of the leather set borrowed over the last few weeks. Speed and stealth weren't as important in this mission, and the metal offered better protection against heavier weapons. A new shield, which was nothing but a circle of wood with a handle, lay on the ground at his feet.

A sharp whistle rose from the rocks several yards further to the north, and Raldus rose just enough to peer out from his hiding place, grateful that the helmet which came with the armor wasn't one of those with a brightly colored plume.

When he looked out, he saw at least a hundred men running full-out toward the town. All of them were wearing faded brown leather breastplates, cingula, and helmets, but no bracers and their sandals only covered their feet. Their weapons were a mixture of short swords, axes, and maces, and only around half of them carried a shield.

Some he could tell had the paler skin of the northern tribes or the darker complexion of Esbera, causing him to briefly wonder why they were all dressed like Naerans.

Raldus watched them long enough to gauge their pace, then slid back down, put his back to the rock and looked up at the eight archers he'd positioned higher up the mountainside. He held up his hand with a single finger raised and the rest hanging loosely, signaling them to nock an arrow.

He counted out ten seconds, then raised a second finger to have them go to half-draw and take aim. The world seemed to stand still as he continued to count, past ten this time and not reacting, even when he heard their running footfalls drawing closer to his position.

Then he finally dropped his arm and the arrows whistled overhead. Shouts and screams rose from the bandits, echoing off the surrounding rocks, and Raldus resisted the urge to smile thinly from the satisfaction it brought him.

He and the other dozen warriors with him rose into a crouch, drew their swords, and picked up their shields as the archers continued shooting. When he looked out at the road again, he saw the bandits running for cover, most of them right toward the waiting warriors.

"Now!" he shouted, and led his men down the slope at their enemy, their training and experience keeping their steps sure on the uneven ground. The bandits pulled up short, most of them raising their weapons to defend themselves, but a few fell backward as they slid to a stop before scrambling back up and taking off toward the fort.

The warriors yelled as they descended, and the archers ceased their volleys to avoid hitting their own people. They would remain there to pick off any exposed targets unless Raldus called them into the melee.

Raldus' first opponent swung a greataxe at his head, but he ducked under and stabbed the man in the gut between armor and belt. When that one went down, Raldus barely had time to stand up and block an overhead sword strike with his shield to get time to bring his sword up again.

He swung his own sword toward the man's torso only to meet with a shield, so he stomped the man's foot, forcing him to drop his guard as he grunted from the pain. When they separated, Raldus brought up his shield and drove into it with his shoulder to knock the man to the ground, at which point he finished him off with a quick slash to the neck.

Two more attacked him, one with a mace and the other with an axe, and he didn't have time to think of history repeating itself as he blocked the mace with his sword and axe with the shield.

The axe bit into the wood and stuck there, so he dropped it and kicked away its owner while he was unbalanced, then parried another blow from the mace. A third strike he swept to the right before reaching out with his left hand, grabbing the man by the throat before kneeing him in the groin, after which he collapsed to the ground holding his hurt with both hands and moaning.

The other one had picked up a different axe from the ground, which he now swung towards Raldus' midsection, who jumped back just in time. Before either of them could attack again, someone grabbed the bandit by the forehead from behind and slit his throat, spraying Raldus with blood before he could spin out of the way.

His helper shoved the man to the ground, revealing himself to be Amili, who simply grunted at Raldus before turning back to the fight, only to find that it was over. More than half the bandits lay on the ground, either writhing in pain or not moving at all. The rest must have fled.

"Our losses?" Raldus called out. Out of the twenty warriors and thirty soldiers who had started the fight, six were dead and eleven more were wounded.

He ordered five of the remaining soldiers to tend to the injured from both sides and for the archers to continue watching the road, then took the rest and jogged to the town to help finish that fight.

Ariela felt nauseous when the first group of wounded came in, their cries of pain and the stench of blood far exceeding anything she'd experienced before. It didn't help when one soldier stumbled in under his own power, then promptly fell to his knees and vomited at her feet, adding to the mix of scents building under the canvas covering.

It was bad, but she swallowed the bile rising in her own throat and removed the man's helmet to reveal a knot on the back of his head, after which he was rushed to a cot by another nurse.

Now she didn't even didn't notice the smells anymore and only paid enough attention to the noise to determine if anyone needed help.

Another group of soldiers rushed into the hospital tent with stretchers holding the injured, and Ariela quickly tied off the bandage wrapped around her current patient's head and rushed over to the new arrivals. Their bearers laid them by the entrance before rushing off again, and she knelt by one with a deep gash in his right arm to first wipe away most of the excess blood with a towel before tightly wrapping the wound with a wine-soaked bandage.

"I haven't seen any of the bandits yet. Are they being treated in another tent?" she asked the older woman who was helping the next man in line.

"They aren't getting any care as ordered by the senate."

"They're killing them!" Ariela gasped, her shock causing her to stop her work for a moment, but she quickly remembered her responsibility and finished applying the bandage.

"Any who don't surrender."

"That's awful," Ariela bemoaned as she moved on to another patient, this one with broken ribs on his left side.

"Spare your pity for people who don't rape, murder, and steal from everyone they come across," the woman snapped.

"No one should be made to suffer."

"There will be much less suffering without people like them in the world."

It was clear there was no getting through this woman's anger and hate, so she almost dropped the subject, but then something else occurred to her.

"What about those who do surrender? What will happen to them?"

"They'll put them on trial and most likely execute them."

"Better be all of them," Ariela's patient moaned as she finished wrapping his ribs.

She chose not to respond any further, but just cupped the man's face reassuringly, then helped carry him to a bed. Yet more patients arrived, and even though she did her best to block out the increase in groans and outright screams of pain, she couldn't help but despair at the suffering and wonder if she was wrong to pity the rebels.

Perhaps everyone truly was better off if those who caused such chaos and pain were not allowed to live.

The sun had yet to reach its zenith when the last group of bandits in the town surrendered. Raldus left the collecting of prisoners to the soldiers and knelt over a dead enemy to use a relatively clean section of the tunic to clean his sword. As he stood again, he slid the sword into its wooden sheath and looked to the north. The rapidly drying fluid splattered over his armor would have to wait until he could sit and clean it properly.

"That was quicker than I expected," Markus commented from his left.

"That was the easy part."

An older warrior approached them with orders from Proclus saying they had half an hour to eat, drink, and/or relieve themselves, then they were to equip for the next phase and go with the others.

"I should return to those I left guarding the road. I'll bring them some rations and you can bring our equipment later," Raldus offered. The older man's puzzled gaze mirrored the looks the warriors had been giving him since his return, a reaction that had grown tiresome. Without a word, he met the man's gaze and patiently awaited a response.

The veteran finally gave his permission with a single nod, and Raldus walked off in search of the supply cart.

"What words of wisdom do you have for me now?" Tallio growled as he watched the runner scramble off down the steps leading away from his quarters.

"A minor defeat only. It happens. Hold fast here and you can still drive them back," the observer replied unironically.

"I noticed that all of your people have left."

"They were only workers and engineers, not soldiers. Construction is complete, so they are no longer needed."

"I still could have used them in the defense."

"This fort is of much higher quality than anything the Naerans have ever faced before. You can defend it with what you have."

"The republic has a history of overcoming more powerful foes," Tallio quietly reasoned in a rare moment of clarity.

"I will remain and assist you if necessary. Even if they should breach the walls, they cannot withstand the power of my staff," the observer encouraged him.

"They never would have gotten this far if you'd destroyed that bridge."

"You know why I did not do so."

"So why would you do anything now?"

The observer sighed as he shifted his weight, lifting the staff slightly in the process and setting it back down with a gentle tap on the gray stone bricks.

"Destroying the bridge would afford them too much insight into my full power and scare them into sending more assets against us. Do not forget that in addition to their own resources, some of which are yet unused, they also have allies whom they have not yet called into any of these fights. I can act here to prevent defeat without causing them to feel as threatened as they would have had I destroyed the bridge and the galley protecting it."

"Trying to figure out when you will or will not act gives me a headache," Tallio confessed as he rubbed his forehead with his right hand.

"Stop trying and trust me to do what is needed," the observer responded, and Tallio looked up at him from beneath the hand.

He made no effort to hide his skepticism, but chose not to speak it aloud. The time would come when he would have to confront this arrogant fool and those for whom he worked, but that wasn't now.

For now, he had a battle to win, and when he did, the whole world would come to know his name.

Chapter Nineteen

No Hiding Place

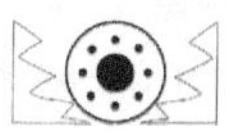

Now that he was looking at the completed fort, Raldus had to wonder who could build something so formidable in so little time, and why they would choose to support a rabble of thugs.

Nestled between two crags going up the slope until they met with a sheer cliff face at the east, it afforded only one avenue of approach. The wall in the front melded with the rocks so well one would think it was naturally occurring if not for the evenly spaced crenellations at the top. They'd carved a short tower directly out of the stone at each end, and a heavy metal portcullis sealed the arched gate at the center.

"I've never seen such engineering anywhere but at Izagion," one of the older warriors gasped.

"And those walls have never been breached," another commented.

"The republic didn't have Stoneforge Warriors fighting with them back then. We'll figure this out," a third boasted. Their words barely registered for Raldus as his thoughts remained on the first comment.

Nobody knew who built the walls and palace at Izagion, not even those currently occupying the city who had admitted long ago that they'd found it after crossing the northern lake in search of game. They claimed the walls and palace were already there, and the rest of the land inside the walls flattened, but it was all abandoned, so they moved in and built the rest of the city as it suited them. There was a legend that it was going to be the home of some god who changed his mind before completion for some reason, but even that failed to name a creator.

The republic suspected the bandits were getting help from someone, but they did not know who. What if it was the same people who built Izagion, either some form of immortal being returned to this world or the descendants of a mortal civilization that was clearly still as advanced?

A low horn sounded, snapping Raldus back to the situation at hand as the army's first line began marching forward. He and the other warriors, along with more soldiers, would go in the second wave.

They did not cheer or shout, and the only sound was of thousands of feet pounding the ground in perfect rhythm as the first wave of nearly a thousand men began marching forward. Those in the front line held their shields close, leaving only their eyes and feet exposed behind the large wooden rectangles. All the others lifted their shields overhead, overlapping them with the one beside and behind them to form a barrier with no gaps large enough for even an arrow to penetrate.

The formation consisted of three cohorts with just over three-hundred in each, the steady cadence of their marching feet and drums echoing off the slopes, one going behind the other until exiting the ravine. The sounds dulled when they reached open ground where the second cohort turned left, briefly increasing its pace to come up beside the first, then the third repeated the maneuver to form the right flank. Each formation moved as one, and each cohort maintained a perfect pace with the others as they crossed the stony ground.

Raldus could just see it as the tiny specks atop the walls ran back and forth before finally forming a single line at the front. Their catapults and ballistae began firing, some of which fell into the gaps between cohorts, but enough found their targets. The weapons were too far away to hear the snap of ropes releasing or creaking of wood, but the thump of rock impacting ground and the startled yelps of soldiers echoed off the mountainside, filling the gorge with the sounds of war. Yet, in all of that, there were no screams of fear, and Raldus couldn't help but admire their courage and take heart for when his own turn came.

The stones crushed shields and toppled soldiers wherever they landed, but the ballista bolts were only effective when they struck the front line directly while any coming down on top bounced off the curved shield ceiling. The soldiers sealed any gaps that opened up by moving into the place of their fallen comrades, and their pace did not slow.

A second horn sounded, signaling their only cavalry to charge. Less than two dozen horsemen thundered into the gaps between the infantry divisions, holding the reins in left hand while lifting a javelin high in the right.

They proved too fast for the poor aim of the defenders and passed through the artillery onslaught without getting hit. Shortly after they were through the barrage, the rebel archers let loose, but made the mistake of aiming instead of showering them with as many arrows as possible. Raldus saw one rider fall, but the rest passed through with no signs of distress.

Within seconds, they reached the wall and let fly their javelins. Their own aim proved far more effective, and most of the catapults stopped as their operators fell to the ground, their screams and the panicky shouts of their comrades replacing the thuds of falling rock and wooden ballista bolts. They thought they were safe behind their fancy new wall, but now they knew better, and Raldus itched to get in there and personally teach them a lesson.

The cavalry circled back as the rebels rushed to replace their fallen and get the catapults working again, but that delay was all the infantry needed to close the distance with a quickened pace.

At a shout from the field officers, the outer cohorts split apart to reveal six ladders in each, which were rushed to the wall and tilted into position. The center formation continued to the gate where they deployed a ram against the steel bars, the dull thud of the regularly spaced impacts reaching back to those waiting to attack.

A third horn sounded after the cavalry returned, and Raldus began marching in sync with the others in the front cohort, the stiffness in his legs from standing for so long swiftly working itself out from the movement. His heartbeat picked up, growing with each step until it felt ready to burst, not out of terror but rather at the prospect of finally finishing this.

There were only two cohorts in this wave, their goal being to get over the walls while the center group from the first dealt with the gate.

Around a hundred and fifty Stoneforge Warriors had gathered for this battle and were mixed with the soldiers in both cohorts. Raldus marched in the second line of the one which took the right flank after reaching open ground. None of the warriors carried shields this time to improve their speed once engaged, so they had to stand behind the soldiers who shielded them all from any remaining projectiles launched at them.

The gate had yet to be breached and the soldiers at the wall were still on the ladders when the second wave entered within range of the enemy artillery, which now targeted them.

"Charge!" the officer ranked Prime, six men down the line from Raldus, shouted seconds after a horn blast sounded from behind.

Both cohorts took off running, and Raldus felt the wind produced by his speed cooling him as the sweat streamed down his face, his breathing remaining steady as his powerful legs drove him forward, even with the weight of the armor which would slow lesser men. They ran past the catapult stones which crashed to the empty ground behind them, but the lower aimed ballista bolts struck their centers, prompting shouts and screams from those they hit until the wooden shafts either shattered or bounced on the stones.

The defenders took too long adjusting their aim for the new speed of their attackers, allowing them to reach the wall without facing another volley. Ready to get into the fight, the warriors shoved their way through the first wave to get to the ladders, and Raldus was no exception. Once at the ladder, he allowed the soldier in front of him to go up, then followed him, choosing to keep his sword sheathed for now.

Each second felt longer than a minute with the warmth rising in Raldus' body from his efforts to wait his turn. The climbers started and stopped several times as those at the top either fought their way off or were pushed back. The shouts and screams from above boiled Raldus' blood further until all he could think about was getting up there and finishing this, even if he had to do it all by himself.

At long last, the soldier in front of him reached the top and stabbed toward a rebel while holding on with his left hand, but his target just ducked beneath the blade and thrust his own into the exposed armpit, killing him instantly.

When he fell, Raldus scrambled up the last few rungs and grabbed the rebel with both hands while hooking his right ankle behind a rung. His opponent swung down and struck him in the back with the pommel of his sword, causing no harm, but the motion shifted the rebel's weight forward, allowing Raldus to pull him out and toss him down the outside of the wall. The weight of all the others on the ladder kept it firmly against the wall.

Leaping onto the wall, he drew his sword in time to slash the throat of another defender rushing at him, then he turned in anticipation of an attack from behind, but there was no need as the next warrior reached over the wall and sliced the man's calf to send him sprawling at Raldus' feet.

Raldus then fought off another opponent, giving the warrior enough time to get off the ladder and enter the fray.

When his latest opponent went down, it created enough of an opening for Raldus to pull a javelin from its strap on his back, after which he threw it at a defender blocking the next ladder down. This turned out to be one of the few rebels wearing a steel breastplate which deflected the javelin with a loud clang when it struck him in the back, but the impact was still enough to send him tumbling off the wall, after which a soldier scrambled into his place.

Within minutes, dozens more warriors and soldiers were atop the wall with the rebels falling before them, the zealous energy of the attackers not leaving them enough time to shout or scream. All that could be heard was the clashing of metal on metal, the thuds of bodies hitting the ground, and grunts from both sides. It didn't take much longer for those remaining to abandon their posts and run off.

Raldus and several others ran to the gate, which showed no signs of damage despite the incessant battering. They slew those defenders unlucky enough to not notice the wall was taken, then raised the portcullis, its chains and bars rattling as it rapidly ascended to grant unrestricted access to the rest of the army.

The soldiers below rushed into the fort, their battle cry sending rebels running deeper inside, and atop the gate, a flag-bearer raised the green Naeran flag with the four wavy horizontal blue lines at its center. A long, low horn sounded at the ravine, confirming their commanders saw the flag and understood they'd breached the wall.

It wouldn't be long now.

"This isn't going well," Tallio growled through gritted teeth. His enemies were already halfway up the slope to his position and showed no signs of slowing or turning back.

"Yes, your men have proven to be most disappointing," the observer remarked softly, and Tallio spun right to face him, but the taller man continued watching the battle with a grim expression.

"What did you expect? A rabble of farmers and townsfolk to defeat an army of soldiers and warriors!"

"I expected more, yes."

"Then you are a fool, after all," Tallio muttered as he looked back at the fighting.

"We drew out their army to fight on multiple fronts. You should have been able to handle what remained with the support we gave."

Every one of Tallio's muscles tensed and his face grew hot, but suddenly all that disappeared as something occurred to him and he calmly focused his gaze on the other man once again.

"Have you people ever actually fought a war before?"

The observer gave him a blank look, then quickly looked away in a reaction one could only interpret as surprise.

So his supporters didn't know what they were doing despite all the power they had shown.

And they'd convinced him to trap himself by this mountain with no means of escape.

He was doomed.

Chapter Twenty

Full Circle

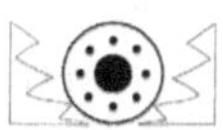

The rebels in the fort fought harder than expected, and kept fighting long after it was clear they could not win. They fought as men more afraid of facing the wrath of their leader than of dying on the blades of their enemies.

It took over two hours for them to get from the wall to the stone stairs at the rear of the fort, but here they were at last. Raldus stood with the tribune and a few others, a mix of warriors and soldiers, and looked up the long staircase at the two men standing there with defiant stares. Only a small portion of their attack force had made it to this point so far, while the rest were still busy fighting any holdouts to secure the rest of the fort.

The man in leather armor Raldus recognized as the bandit leader, Tallio Atroni, the man who had stood back and laughed while his men nearly killed him all those months ago, but the other one was unlike anyone he had ever seen before. He stood to Tallio's right, which showed him to be much taller, his skin was the color of bronze, and he wore dark blue armor of a strange alloy that covered his entire body save his head. In his right hand he held a golden staff topped by a diamond-shaped figure, the whole thing standing at the same height as him with its bottom placed on the ground.

"You're defeated! Surrender!" the tribune called out.

"Never!" Tallio refused as he drew his sword.

"You can't fight us!"

"How little you know," the man next to Tallio observed as he lifted his staff and pointed it at the tribune.

A beam of red light shot out of the diamond tip with a loud crackling sound and struck the tribune square in the chest, sending him flying back while the rest of the group shielded their eyes and recoiled from the sudden intense heat.

When Raldus turned, he saw the tribune flat on his back several yards away from where he'd been standing with a thin tendril of smoke curling up above his heart. One soldier rushed to him, only to pull back as he stared at the body with mouth agape.

They looked back up the stairs to see both Tallio and the stranger watching them with insidious smiles. Now that they had everyone's attention again, the stranger pointed his staff at a warrior, causing him and the rest of the group to scatter as the beam passed between them.

A collection of rocks adjacent to the stairs offered a semblance of protection. That sense of security was shattered when the beam struck a rock, blasting it into pieces. Those crouching behind it were violently thrown to the ground, their hands instinctively covering their faces as they cried out in pain, their bodies trembling as they rocked back and forth.

Three more soldiers jogged up from the lower fort toward them, only for all three to be cut down in a single blast.

"Malius, protect me!" the warrior next to Raldus cried out to the god of heroes before darting out of cover. His speed was impressive, getting him up three steps before the beam struck him in the gut and sent him back to the bottom where he lay doubled up. A low moan rose from the man as his legs partially straightened and contracted, then he went limp and fell silent.

Raldus poked his head up enough to see over the rock at the same time a soldier near him and a warrior from across the stairs ran out. He saw Tallio laugh as both were struck down, first the warrior, then the soldier.

The space between the crags framing the fort narrowed at this point, leaving a few yards between them and the stairs through which someone could run up to avoid the steps altogether, but there was no cover to be had and anyone attempting it would be dead there as surely as on the stairs.

He slid back down and leaned his back against the rock, closing his eyes and tuning out the continuing carnage as his mind raced to find a solution. The soldier next to him kept mumbling prayers to various deities, from Keslu, king of the gods, to Sarias, god of war, begging for his life to be spared. Unable to think of a way past this incredible weapon, Raldus decided it couldn't hurt to risk trusting a higher power himself. The last time he trusted only in himself resulted in failure, after all.

"I speak to Rosjen, whom I have been told is the one true god made manifest. Your followers claim that you are always with us and always hear our prayers," he whispered to the god worshiped by Ariela and her people. He felt ridiculous, but pushed ahead anyway.

"If this is true, hear me now. Grant me the power to end this conflict, to end all this death. Show me the way," he concluded. It occurred to him he should promise to devote the rest of his life to this god in return for this favor, but he knew he wasn't ready to do such a thing and his honor prevented him from making a promise he couldn't, or wouldn't, keep.

Opening his eyes, he looked around to see that the beam was now being aimed over the rocks, which effectively kept the attackers pinned down, but did nothing to hurt them unless they were stupid enough to expose themselves. If it was capable of blasting apart their cover, why didn't the stranger do it and be rid of them?

Two men not part of the original group had joined them and taken cover next to what remained of the destroyed stone, but none of the shots were being directed at them even when one of them stood up enough to throw a javelin. A brave move, but the weapon was shot out of the air halfway to its target.

The one who threw it returned to his cover without facing retaliation. It seemed as if the stranger was avoiding targeting them, but why? Then Raldus noticed a cloud of dust above their heads sparkling in the sunlight, and he couldn't help but wonder if that was what was being avoided, as ridiculous a notion as it seemed.

He couldn't see any way to close the distance without everyone who tried getting killed, and they would not retreat to let this evil overrun their land, so even the most absurd of ideas was worth a try. Making sure to stay in cover, he rotated onto his right hip, gathered a few loose stones in his left hand, then pulled himself up into a crouch.

He paused in that stance to think of Ariela, refreshing his spirit with the desire to see her again. She was all that he had vowed to protect in this world, and that was worth seeing again.

"Fire of spirit," he whispered, gathering further strength from the last line of his creed, then he launched himself out of cover and ran as far as the center of the stairs before stopping to face his adversaries.

The stranger aimed his staff at him, his own gaze neutral while Tallio watched with a gleeful grin, and Raldus tossed the stones into the beam's path right as it activated.

The beam struck them and dispersed in a spectacular burst of light as they exploded into a cloud of dust. After his eyes recovered from the flash, Raldus looked up to see the stranger angrily glaring at him, while Tallio merely looked confused.

"Now!" Raldus shouted as he charged up the stairs. The others let out a mighty roar and followed, swarming all over the steps.

Upon reaching the spot where the stones had intercepted the beam, Raldus spotted some which were still intact and scooped them up. The stranger took aim at him, determined to reacquire his advantage. However, the warrior carefully observed the man's eyes and anticipated the moment he would shoot, then hurled the stones directly at the staff.

This time, they met the beam mere inches from its source, and when they exploded, tiny tendrils of lightning snaked around the staff, forcing the stranger to drop it with a loud hiss to hold his right hand in his left.

Right before the attackers could reach him, he grabbed the staff with his left hand and took off running while Tallio stood there looking between him and the others.

Half of the soldiers and warriors pursued the stranger while Raldus and the rest circled around the rebel leader, who held them back with a raised sword. The weapon no longer shone in the sunlight as it had when Raldus owned it, but its condition hardly mattered to him now.

"You!" he blurted when his gaze settled upon Raldus.

"So you do remember me."

"I killed you!"

"No, you thought your men killed me while you did nothing. There's no one for you to hide behind now," Raldus countered in a calm, even tone.

"So you're here to return the favor and have me fight all these men at once, is that it?"

"No," Raldus replied simply, receiving surprised glances from many in the group.

"Oh, you must be one of those who thinks it makes you a better person to forego revenge and arrest me instead," Tallio spat.

"I didn't say that."

"Then what *are* you going to do?" the man exclaimed as his green eyes burned with anger and hate.

"I challenge you to single combat."

The bandit leader roared with laughter as Raldus patiently waited for him to finish.

"And I suppose if I win, the rest of them are just going to let me go?" Tallio questioned, jerking his head to the right to indicate all the others still surrounding him.

"I don't speak for them. My goal is to finish what I started, and I don't care what they do afterward."

"Why would I accept this?"

"You get to go down fighting, and if you do win, you get to take at least one of us down with you.".

The bandit thought about it for a moment, then grinned wide and said, "So be it."

Raldus stepped up to him, struck a fighting pose with his right foot forward and knees slightly bent, and placed the flat of his blade against that of his opponent's while the others all stepped back to give them room, including those who had just arrived.

"This time, you die for real, and on your own sword, no less," Tallio taunted, but Raldus ignored him.

Tallio snarled as he lunged forward with sword point aimed at his opponent's face, but Raldus ducked to the right, parrying the sword in the same motion while also sticking out a foot to trip the bandit. It worked, and Tallio sprawled forward onto the ground as Raldus brought his sword down in an arc towards his neck, but Tallio rolled into his legs to send him crashing to the ground before the blow could land.

Raldus fell on his opponent, who swiftly escaped but was immediately struck in the face with a kick. He retaliated by driving an elbow into Raldus' thigh, the latter then rolling away from him. This gave Tallio enough space to get to his feet and come after him swinging his sword.

Still on his back, Raldus blocked the strike and kicked out to land a blow on the man's left shin, knocking him off-balance long enough for the warrior to use an elbow to push himself backward along the ground before climbing to his feet.

Screaming in rage, Tallio advanced on him, wildly swinging his sword in wide slashes, but Raldus calmly dodged each one as he backed away. In a daring move, he dropped his sword, and when his opponent swung down again, he grabbed Tallio's right wrist and held that arm down while driving his elbow into the man's bearded face.

The blow stunned him, causing his grip to loosen, and Raldus yanked the sword from his grasp and slashed it across his chest, doing no damage thanks to the leather breastplate, but still forcing him back and creating space between them.

He then got a proper grip on the stolen sword, grabbed the man by a shoulder before he could recover his balance, and thrust the sword into his gut under his armor and angled up toward his heart.

The man's eyes bulged in pain, then clouded over and Raldus pushed him to the ground with the sword still in him.

Not uttering a single word, he casually stooped down and retrieved the sword he'd brought with him, wiped off any remaining blood on his own tunic, then sheathed it and walked away.

Chapter Twenty-One

Shallow Dreams, Deep Wisdom

Ariela stood by the fountain at Naera's north gate watching the returning soldiers and warriors, wondering if Raldus would be among them this time. It had been over a month since the battle to retake that one town and clear the rebel fort, during which time the wounded and those caring for them had returned to the city while the army and warriors broke into smaller units to search the countryside for any holdouts. Most of the camps they found were abandoned, and those few rebels they did find were easily arrested.

The latest news from Elder Proclus was that most of the warriors had gone up north during the last three weeks to fight the wild tribes or to Esbera in the east to assist in that war. He didn't know where Raldus was or if he intended to join one of those groups, only that he was unharmed and assisting in the efforts as he saw fit.

She was confident he wouldn't leave her behind without at least telling her when, or if, to expect him, but she hadn't seen him since before the battle and had no way of knowing if it had changed him. She'd heard the monks speak about how anger and vengeance can corrupt a soul, and she wondered what Raldus was feeling and thinking now that he'd confronted and killed the man who nearly destroyed him.

Then there he was, the last to come through the gate. He looked around, spotted her, and walked up to her as he smiled wearily with a genuine warmth beneath the fatigue.

"It's over. There are no more bandits, or rebels, whatever you want to call them now," he revealed upon reaching her.

"What now?"

"I have to report to Elder Proclus, then speak with a deputy to confirm that my service is complete and is enough to pay the tax for your town, then I will be taking you home."

"Oh," she uttered as she broke eye contact to look at the ground.

So much had happened, and she'd been so busy at the hospital that thoughts of home had scarcely occurred to her. Now that she was thinking about it again, she hoped everyone was doing well and she dearly missed them all, but she wasn't sure she was ready to go back. There was still so much to see and learn.

"That won't be for a few days yet. The fighting actually goes by quicker than the bureaucracy," he assured her as if he knew exactly what was going through her mind.

She looked back at him to see him studying her, and she offered a weak smile in response.

"I suppose I should let you get to it then," she told him, then turned to leave, but he blocked her way with his arm.

"I'd like for you to walk with me for a while," he revealed. She nodded her agreement and the two of them headed for the center of the city.

"It may take longer, but at least nobody gets hurt," she observed in an attempt to start a conversation.

"Politics are anything but painless," he joked, then smiled at her lighthearted laugh.

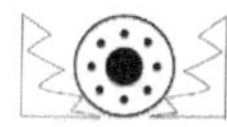

How could I have ever wanted such things? Raldus thought as he looked over the raucous crowd from his position behind the table on the stage.

He had hoped to be out of the city by now, but the senate had declared a festival in honor of their victory over the rebels and refused to release him from his contract unless he attended. So here he sat, feasting and drinking in the main plaza lit by dozens of torches, while others continued to fight and die in the other conflicts.

To his left at the table's center seat was the consul, the republic's leader as elected by the senate, and on his other side sat a tribune recently promoted to replace the one slain in the battle for the fort. Normally the legate, the army's top commander, would occupy that seat, but he was currently in Esbera overseeing the war.

Four more men sat on either side of those three, a mix of senators and army officers. They were on the plaza's eastern stage since the senate building was on the river's east bank at the location where legend said their ancestors chose to build the city, or the gods, depending on which story a person believed. Each of the other three stages featured a different form of entertainment with musicians on the north, acrobats on the south, and thespians portraying their final victory on the west.

Around the shrine honoring Keslu and Livaria at the center were tables laden with food and drink while men in togas and women in dresses, both equally colorful, meandered around the open spaces. He'd heard how wild such parties often became, so Raldus had insisted Ariela remain at the inn.

The consul, a middle-aged man with an athletic build and short black hair, stood up and straightened his blue toga and purple sash. When he was satisfied with his image, he held out his golden cup which prompted the horn-blowers to sound their call from each side of the stage, silencing and summoning the people with the deep tone that reverberated off the stones and rolled down the torch lit city streets.

"People of ill intent have terrorized our land for many months, stealing our goods, murdering our people, raping our women, and selling our children into slavery. Much blood was spilled to end this evil, and tonight we celebrate the restoration of peace and safety to our great republic!" the consul spoke, then took a long sip of wine as the people cheered.

Those at the table rose and joined in the toast, including Raldus, even though he wished he could be anywhere else right now. How had he ever thought he would enjoy this kind of life?

When they had sat back down, the consul turned and held out his wineglass to him specifically.

Now what was he going to do?

"One man in particular suffered much in the quest to destroy the one who dared attempt to make himself your king. Raldus Velix nearly died hunting down the traitor Tallio Atroni when few others took the threat he posed seriously, but he returned stronger than ever to save us in our time of great need."

The crowd cheered again while Raldus clenched his jaw to keep himself from correcting the consul with his political spin on the tale. He did not deny that he had done a great deal, but even so, his part was rather small compared to the scale of the conflict.

"He fought these criminals in their camps, entered their territory to spy on them, and formed the strategy which ultimately defeated them. When no one else was able to find a way past their final defense to reach their leader, he did. Then he confronted this man who had presumed himself strong enough to kill a warrior of the mighty Stoneforge order and ended his reign of terror once and for all!"

More cheers, which lasted twice as long as the previous instance, and the consul waited patiently as he watched the crowd with a massive smile, his face flushed both from the wine and the adulation his words incited.

"For these mighty deeds, I proposed, and the senate approved, to name him, Raldus Velix, Champion of the Republic!"

The crowd applauded and shouted their approval as the consul held out his cup to the seated warrior.

It was the highest honor the republic could bestow to a veteran, whether he was a soldier or a warrior. Normally it took someone a lifetime of service to earn the title, and oftentimes it was only conferred after death during the funeral. This was what he'd sought his entire life, but not even in his wildest dreams had he dared to imagine it would come to him at his young age.

Now that it was here, he found himself divided in his feelings. At first, his mind flooded with images of him returning home dressed in the finest clothes money could buy and riding a magnificent steed proclaiming how he'd proven all their doubts wrong. They could perform great deeds, get recognized for them, and still follow the code.

Then his gut knotted as the memory of his first encounter with Tallio and his bandits shattered the daydream. He had approached Tallio and his gang of bandits in the forest, confident nothing could stop him, and that arrogance had nearly gotten him killed. Then he reflected on all the suffering that had to happen to so many people for this moment to even be possible, and for the first time in his life he finally understood why most interpreted the code to mean they were only to earn what they needed to live without pursuing fame or riches.

Their calling was to fight, to face danger and keep others safe. A warrior could not seek glory without courting that danger, compromising the safety of others in the process and thus failing in their purpose.

He glanced at Elder Proclus standing at the front of the crowd watching him with an unreadable expression. The consul had invited him to sit at the table next to Raldus, but he had politely refused. Guessing at the elder's current thoughts, Raldus swallowed hard, then stood up and looked at the consul ready to refuse the honor but hesitated when he saw the man's expectant look and he realized it would be a bad idea to outright reject the offer and embarrass him in front of the people.

So he did the only thing he could and grasped the consul's left arm just below the elbow and the leader returned the action.

"I accept this honor on behalf of all who fought to return safety to our land and in remembrance of all the heroes who gave their lives for the cause," he declared loud enough for all to hear.

The consul smiled even wider, drained his cup, then gave Raldus' arm a firm shake before releasing it and slamming his cup onto the table. They both turned to face the enthusiastic applause of the crowd, and Raldus looked at Proclus to see that even he was respectfully clapping. When their eyes met, the elder gave him a single approving nod accompanied by a half-smile.

This lasted until the consul raised his arms above his head and spread them wide to make his next announcement.

"I name you Raldus Velix Praelior, Champion of the Republic, Protector of the People!"

A final cheer rose from the people, their voices combining into one to resound through the city and rise to the stars themselves.

Chapter Twenty-Two

Homecoming

The trip back to Our Sacred Refuge, the name given for both the monastery and town together, was somehow more eventful in safer times than when they had traveled to the city while the bandits were ravaging the countryside.

Raldus had left the golden circlet and ruby pin, symbols of the champion, with Elder Proclus, but word had raced ahead of them of the Stoneforge Warrior who had rid the land of the menace that had plagued it. The roads were full of travelers rushing to sell their goods and buy supplies for the approaching winter, and it seemed each of them had to stop and shower him with praise. Each time, Ariela had to step aside, unseen by all but her companion, who often looked at her apologetically over the heads of his fans.

This continued even after he stopped the tough guy act and put on a warmer tunic with long sleeves which covered the tattoo on his right forearm. However, he could not hide his warrior physique, causing people to ask if he was the one who was now their champion, and his honor compelled him to answer truthfully. One question he did tire of answering was why he hadn't gone on to fight in Esbera or the north, and after a while his response was simply to shrug it off.

One time, a man pushed her to the ground to get to Raldus, begging his blessing. In a flash of anger that shocked her with its intensity, the warrior grabbed the front of the man's tunic with both hands and threw him into the ditch, then offered her a hand up as he glared at the startled supplicant. After she was back on her feet and had dusted herself off, they turned their backs on the man still sitting there and walked away without a word. He did not pursue them, possibly fearing for his life.

Because of all this, it had taken them an extra day to get as far as the forest, but at least once they were on the path, they finally found themselves alone. Now they were but minutes from the gate, and had walked this far without talking, each of them grateful for the silence in a way the other understood without speaking it aloud.

"Have any of your feelings about your faith changed with all you've seen?" Raldus suddenly asked.

Her surprise at the question left her speechless at first, and she delayed by looking ahead at where the wall and its entrance would appear at any moment. She recalled the memories of her life there, free from the violence of men but full of other struggles. Storms had destroyed their homes, summer droughts left them short on food over the winter, and many had died in accidents or to the occasional wild animal that found its way past their walls.

It was easy to think that these things did not compare to all the pain and misery she'd seen over the last few weeks, but she knew in her heart it was all the same, only the source was different. Such things were a part of life and all one could do was endure it and continue living to the best of their ability.

"If you're asking me if my beliefs have changed, the answer is no. All that has changed is that I feel a stronger connection to my Lord, and I better understand how much he is needed in this world. I also feel that we, that I, can't keep hiding here and should be out there helping people," she finally responded.

He only nodded thoughtfully and said nothing more.

"Have these events affected your beliefs?" she asked after a few seconds.

"I don't know yet," he told her as the stone gateway came into view. She chose not to press the matter and the two of them went through to find a teenage boy in a white wool shirt and brown trousers sitting on the other side. When he saw them, he launched himself to his feet, sending the chair clattering to the stones, and ran off into the plaza.

"She's here! Ariela's back! She lives!" the boy cried as he ran. Any nearby monks hurried up to gush over Ariela, repeatedly telling how happy they were to see their prayers answered with her returning to them safe and sound.

More came out of the buildings to replace the first wave of greeters as the boy's cries faded down the hill toward the town. It was all she could do to assure them she was unharmed and treated well by those she had encountered. She could barely get two words out before someone else showed up to repeat questions already asked and throw new ones at her.

"That's enough," a deep voice finally cut through the chaos, saving her rapidly deteriorating voice. The crowd parted to reveal Abbot Jerald, who smiled warmly as he walked up and clasped both her hands between his.

"Thank you, Abbot," she told him after lowering her gaze.

"Ariela!"

At the sound of her father's voice, her gaze snapped up again to see him running full out across the plaza toward her. The elderly abbot barely had enough time to get out of his way as he swooped in and wrapped her up in both arms.

"I'm so glad you're home," he whispered, sounding on the verge of tears.

"Thank you, Father. It's good to be back," she gasped, using what little air she could manage within his tight embrace.

When he finally let her go, he held her out in front of him with a hand on each of her shoulders to look her up and down, then he looked over to her left and smiled warmly.

“Thank you for keeping my daughter safe,” he said, and she followed his gaze to see Raldus standing just inside the gate watching the scene with an expression mixing amusement and confusion. His only response was to give Imri a respectful nod.

“He did more than keep me safe,” Ariela started to say, but Raldus cut her off.

“That’s not important right now,” he said with a look demanding her silence on his feats.

“Yes, now is the time for celebration. Tonight we celebrate the safe return of she who ventured out to tend the hurting,” Jerald declared, and she followed with the crowd to help with the preparations, no matter their objections.

The monks and townspeople who had made it wandered toward the stairs leading to the town below, but Raldus stayed at the entrance as Ariela went with them. Perhaps it would be for the best if he just turned around and left right now.

“I sense there is something on your mind,” Jerald observed, getting him to look over at the old man who was still there for some reason.

“Here is your armor, mended and polished. My gratitude to you for its use,” the warrior said as he swung the bundle from his shoulder and held it out, dropping his supply sack in the process, but the abbot waved it away with his right hand.

“No, it is yours now. You have earned it,” he stated, surprising Raldus both with the refusal and by not calling out his obvious ducking of the implied question.

They looked at each other over the bundle as he continued to hold it out, him debating what he should do next while Jerald looked on with a knowing smile which both calmed the youth with its warmth while also infuriating him with its hidden meaning.

"Come, join us," Jerald invited before walking away across the plaza. Raldus watched him a moment, then swung the bundle back over his shoulder, picked up the sack, and followed.

"Tonight, we give thanks for the safe return of one of our cherished townspeople, Ariela fret Imri," Jerald announced after everyone had gathered and the excited conversation quieted down.

From his position at the front of the forum, he looked out over the people standing by the tables which had been set up for this occasion, feeling his heart warmed by their smiles. Then he looked down at the nineteen-year-old girl still seated at his right who was currently blushing and staring at the table between the plate of food and glass of wine. Next to her sat her father, Imri, and younger brother, Tobias, both of them with proud gazes fixed upon her.

"Her concern for the safety of another was more powerful than any desires she felt for herself, leading her to join him on a perilous journey to see to his needs. Such is the love of our Lord Rosjen which he calls all of us to exemplify," he continued while smiling down at her.

He placed an encouraging hand on her shoulder, and she looked up at him long enough to give him an embarrassed, but genuinely pleasant, smile.

Then he linked his hands within their sleeves over his stomach, glanced down at Raldus on his left who was calmly watching him, and finally looked back at the crowd.

"We also find ourselves owing gratitude to a young man who came to us many months ago as a stranger in need of our help and proved to be the right person in the right place at the right time to help us. He prevented the ransacking of our homes by offering himself in service to pay what we could not, and he returned Ariela's care with protection. His skills are now tempered by wisdom, and I foresee more great deeds in his future," Jerald described. The attendees clapped politely, and he waited for them to finish before calling them to bow their heads in prayer.

"Great and Merciful God, we thank you for watching over Ariela on her journey and returning her to us unharmed in body and mind. We pray that her presence blessed those she met as much as it has always blessed us, and may the love she showed others reflect back upon you and reveal you to those who know you not. Thank you for sending Raldus to us for the moment you knew he would be needed, and may your wisdom continue to grace him so he may become as strong of mind as he is of body and spirit. We also praise you for a fruitful harvest this year, making this celebration feast possible. In the name of our Lord Rosjen, all truth."

"All truth," Keid echoed the benediction along with everyone present, then looked at the head table to see if Raldus reacted to the speech and prayer at all, but instead focused on Jerald as he walked away after bidding everyone to eat.

Curious about this behavior, Keid politely excused himself from the table and followed the abbot. The old man was slow but strong as he treaded the path and ascended the stairs to the monastery proper, then around the main building and down the stairs to the garden. Near the middle, where a wall of rock and dirt connected to the hill upon which sat the main building, he paused long enough to push aside some ferns to reveal an opening in the rock into which he promptly entered.

Keid approached the ferns, waited a minute to ensure the movement wouldn't be noticed, then pushed them back and ducked into the tunnel lit by a single torch where it turned to the left a few yards ahead.

The tunnel was a short one, so after turning the corner, he exited mere seconds later into the secret garden known only to the fully initiated. He looked around and spotted Jerald sitting in a wood chair by the pool and staring at the reflection of the stars in the water.

"It is not like you to walk away from your people, Abbot. What is on your mind that vexes you so?" Keid quietly asked after walking up to stand beside him.

"If I desired to share my thoughts with someone, you are the last one I would consider for the responsibility," Jerald snapped.

So much for the kind and respectful approach.

"Perhaps you are finally coming to understand that not all outsiders are bad people, that they are worthy of our respect and we have much to offer them," the monk retorted, then turned to leave without awaiting a response. However, even in his present mood, the abbot was not one to let someone else have the last word.

"Or perhaps I've heard enough of what they endured to have good reason to worry about who will be seeking us out next."

The monk halted, ready to throw something back at the old man, but decided he wasn't in the mood to argue and left to return to the party instead.

Chapter Twenty-Three

The Future Calls

Her first morning back home saw Ariela resuming her old routine by rising before the sun to prepare breakfast for her family. The fire had died down during the night, so she added a red shawl over her dress for extra warmth.

She sneaked into the main room, her bare feet silent on the chilly wood floor, so as not to disturb Raldus. Her father had insisted he stay with them instead of at the monastery, but she discovered his bedroll rolled up and placed neatly in a corner. Apparently, he decided to leave during the night and avoid any farewells.

Swallowing her disappointment, she held her chin up and marched into the kitchen, intent on not letting her sadness disrupt her work, if she allowed herself to feel it at all. If he decided he didn't have any reason to stay, who was she to disagree?

The sun would warm the house soon enough, so she omitted stoking the fire and started by putting away the various plates, utensils, and pot left out on the tables. She supposed she couldn't complain too much because at least they were all clean.

All else went like normal, almost as if she had never left, and shortly after sunrise her father and brother were out in the field and she was on her way to the forum to help clean up from the night before. No one said a word about Raldus, causing her to wonder if she was to just return to her life and forget about him and the events of the last few months.

Upon reaching the forum, she discovered some others had already started, a mix of younger monks from the monastery, women from the town, and one man in a white tunic carrying a small table by himself. The tunic stood out in stark contrast to the women's dresses of varying shades of brown and the gray robes of the monks, and when she spotted it, she froze in place, wondering if she dared think it was who she thought.

It couldn't have been anyone else, a fact proven when he set the table down and turned toward her to reveal the weathered face which had become so familiar to her.

In a rush of emotion, she ran up to him, but caught herself at the last second and stopped short as he stood there looking at her. Her face grew warm, and she looked down in an attempt to hide her embarrassment while clearing her throat to buy some time.

"You weren't there for breakfast."

"I couldn't sleep, so I went for a walk, then joined the others when they started working."

"Is there something wrong?" she asked, meeting his gaze.

"There are many things on my mind, that is all."

She accepted his assurance there was nothing inadequate about her family's hospitality with a nod, then looked down at the stones again.

"I thought you'd left," she admitted.

"Not yet. Maybe never. I haven't decided yet," he responded dispassionately.

Her heart raced at the words, and she looked into his eyes again as the hope she'd been resisting burst inside her. Despite his indifferent demeanor, she could see a softness creeping into his features, threatening to melt the harshness he was used to presenting to the world.

"Where else would you go?" she demurred.

His response was to shrug and look off into the distance as if picturing the whole world in his mind, his face tinged with sadness.

"If you think you don't have a home anywhere, perhaps it is time to make one," she suggested. He looked back down at her and held her eyes with his own as a slight smile worked its way across his lips.

"I'll keep that in mind," he promised, and she returned the smile tenfold. They held each other's gaze for a few more seconds, then they nodded in silent understanding and walked away from the stacked tables and chairs. One of the older women handed her a broom, and all of them gave her shrewd smiles but didn't speak their thoughts aloud. She took the broom to sweep up the dirt and crumbs while trying to ignore the heat rising in her face once again.

As she worked, it occurred to her that neither of them had expressed any feelings aloud, nor treated the other as anything but a friend. Yet, the bond which started before their adventure had grown undeniably deep during those events, and they did not require words to know what they had come to mean to one another.

She stole a glance at him over the broom handle, smiling as he helped a monk struggling to lift a table, but her breath seized in her throat upon remembering her duty to her people and their beliefs.

Was it even possible for the two of them to have a life together?

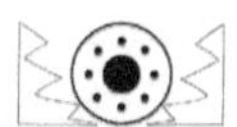

"The land is safe once more, and it won't be long now before the Esberans and northern tribes are defeated," Raldus finished his report to Jerald and Keid from his position standing in front of the former's desk. The diffused light coming through the red and blue window behind them, plus the candlelight from the three-pronged stand behind Raldus, served to cast the room in a soft glow. This, combined with the peaceful quiet, created a rather eerie atmosphere given the intensity of the events he'd described.

It was odd to see these two together, but he had no interest in guessing at the complexities of their feud.

Both had asked the occasional question during his relating of the events since he left the monastery, but for the most part, they had sat in silence and let him tell it how he desired.

"When you came to us, you believed yourself capable of taking on any challenge. You knew you were destined for greatness. It appears you were right," Jerald remarked, causing Raldus to stand taller and smile as pride swelled his heart. Then he looked at their faces and realized it was not a compliment since both of them wore stern expressions, even the normally warm and sympathetic Keid.

Then he deflated a little, looked at the floor, and reminded himself of what was truly important, which he then spoke aloud.

"The people are safe. That is what matters."

"And you are their hero, as you should be."

"What do you want to hear, old man?" Raldus challenged as he tensed up and looked the abbot in the eye again.

"The truth about the nature of who stands before me now. Has he grown into a man, or does he remain a child?"

The warrior glanced at Keid, who showed no support within his stern features, then he looked back at Jerald and swallowed hard as he fought to find the right thing to say.

"I don't have an answer for you. I am not who I was, and I don't recognize myself now."

The two monks glanced at each other, shared some silent understanding, and when they looked back at him, their expressions had softened somewhat.

"You said that when you and the others were trapped by this weapon, you prayed to our god for guidance. Why?" Keid spoke up.

"It seemed like a good idea at the time."

"But why our god? Why not one worshiped by your own people?"

He shrugged, but both of his interviewers kept watching him expectantly, so he looked down and thought back to that moment. As he followed this line of thought, it led him through his entire life, from childhood up to that moment in the battle.

"I've never seen anyone benefit from praying to those beings, only stories spread by the priests. With the people here I saw something different, a feeling which persisted with Ariela's company. When it comes down to it, it seemed pointless to go to any of them but harmless to try a new one," he finally explained as best he could.

"Even while not believing in him," Jerald accused.

"Nothing else was working, so like I said, it was worth a try," Raldus shot back.

"A try that seems to have worked out," Keid suggested, eliciting another shrug from the warrior.

"You have a decision to make," Jerald declared.

"What do you mean?"

"You have seen and learned much, too much to feign your former ignorance. It is time to decide between continuing in disbelief, or choosing a path of faith."

"You're telling me I have to convert," Raldus accused as he tensed up once again.

"That has always been our goal, one which we have never hidden from you, but the choice is yours," Keid interjected.

He glared at both of them as every childhood argument with his father, instructors, and other veterans ran through his head, his blood boiling more and more with each memory. All his life he'd hated being told what to believe, and that was one thing that hadn't changed.

Unable to contain himself any longer, he clenched his fists at his sides and stared both of them down.

"I don't have to do anything," he growled, then turned and stormed off.

As he stomped through the halls, he wondered if he was truly angry at them for demanding a decision, or at himself for not having made one.

The thought only enraged him further, leading him to throw open the main doors and nearly knock down a monk as he headed for his training area which the monks had left intact.

"Why is this so difficult a matter to decide?" Keid asked Raldus, confronting the young man on his way out the gate with a short bow in hand and quiver of arrows on his back. He'd been avoiding the monks since the challenge to convert three days ago, and Keid was tired of waiting for him to start a conversation.

"Leave me alone," Raldus grunted as he kept walking, but the monk stepped into his path.

"Only if you give me a proper answer," he challenged.

The warrior's green eyes flashed with anger, but Keid did not budge, then Raldus sighed and looked past him with unfocused eyes.

"I must be sure that any decision I make is for the right reasons," he admitted, his tone solemn.

"Why else would you convert if you do not believe?" Keid questioned, his own voice now soft and understanding.

All Raldus did in response was to droop his head and avert his gaze as if looking at something behind him in his periphery.

Keid looked behind him, spotted a thin trail of smoke rising from the town, then smiled upon realizing where a young man's thoughts often dwelt.

"You are an honorable man who would never make a vow in which you did not believe, even if that vow is necessary for another upon which you've already decided," he remarked, then stepped aside.

He smiled warmly when Raldus met his gaze, and the young man nodded his respect.

After Raldus proceeded through the gate, the monk continued to stand there, gazing at the empty space with an amused smile as he thought of his god's subtle workings in their lives.

As she approached the eastern pool, a full clothes basket held out in front of her, Ariela cast a curious glance at the other women grouped together as far as possible from the stone wall closing off the monk's garden. There was so little room between them that they kept bumping into each other as they dunked and rinsed their laundry, but they did not attempt to separate.

Some of them looked up long enough to acknowledge her, then continued with their work without saying anything. Seeing no reason to subject herself to the same discomfort, or add to theirs, she kept walking to find a better spot. When she was just a few feet away, the sound of raised voices from the garden startled her into stopping in her tracks.

It wasn't unusual for the monks to have some spirited discussions on matters of doctrine and certain practices, but they rarely fought to the point of shouting at one another. She glanced back at the other workers to see that the younger ones had stopped and were now watching her with intense interest while the older women continued working without a care.

She should probably go back to them, but her curiosity got the better of her and she proceeded down the edge of the water until she could make out the words.

"We are called to share the hope of our Lord to all people, not hide away in false safety!" Keid's familiar voice declared as she set down the basket and removed her sandals.

"*False* safety! Is that what you call the last hundred years of no one trying to kill us!" Abbot Jerald's voice shot back in response as she waded knee deep into the water, her dress growing heavy from the water it soaked up.

"Only because they decided we're more trouble than we're worth!"

"So you would have us give them reason to think otherwise!"

"I would have us do our duty as followers of Rosjen! The people of this nation need to hear what he offers, and this man proves it!"

"The change in the life of a single young man months after nearly getting himself killed doesn't prove anything!" Jerald argued.

Apparently, Raldus was also with them, though she was yet to hear his voice.

"It proves that there are people ready to listen, and we are doing them a disservice by not showing them the way!"

No response this time.

The only sound was the soft splashing of the water as she took out or added an item.

She knew Raldus had been meeting with the two monks over the past few days, usually one or the other, sometimes together, but she didn't know about what, since the two of them had seen very little of each other in that time. The argument she was now hearing was an old one, which seemed to have taken on new fervor from his continued presence. His part in it remained a mystery.

"That's enough for now. We will discuss this again later," Jerald's weary voice finally concluded, so quietly that she had to strain to understand the words.

They said nothing more, not that she could hear anyway, leaving her to presume that they had all agreed to end the discussion for now.

Chapter Twenty-Four

New Life

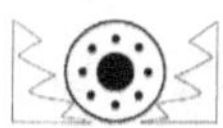

The heat rising from the stones mixed with that of the noon sun to bring a welcome warmth within the chilly day. Raldus looked over the townspeople gathered in the forum before him, and took a deep breath before speaking.

"I have come to believe, through personal experience and deep consideration, that Rosjen is the one true God made flesh who came to redeem us and show us the path to eternal life," he announced, prompting loud applause from the crowd.

He looked at Ariela standing with her father and brother in the front row and felt himself warmed by her wide smile and misty eyes. They held each other's gaze as Abbot Jerald spoke his piece from Raldus' right.

"After much discussion, I am convinced that he has truly accepted this in his heart and have anointed him in the faith as witnessed by a gathering of the monks."

"I have learned why you formed this sanctuary, and why you continue to fear those outside these walls. It is my hope to be a bridge between you and them so that Rosjen's light may shine for all to see," Raldus disclosed upon returning his attention to the crowd, thankful to Keid for giving him the words to say. He had expected his friend to be up here with him, but suspected Jerald had prevented it. The two may be starting to work together, but there was still much animosity between them.

"We will work with him in his mission outside these walls, teaching him what he needs to know and providing shelter as needed or desired. At times, one or more of our order may join him if they should choose to do so," the abbot promised, his voice straining and almost failing with the last sentence. It was never easy for someone to admit they may have been, or actually were, wrong.

This revelation sparked whispers among the crowd, some excited, others fearful, but none objected.

With nothing else to be said, the abbot bade them to bow their heads, then said a prayer thanking God for Raldus' change of heart and asking for his wisdom to guide them throughout the coming efforts.

When he finished, he dismissed the assembly, and Raldus looked again at Ariela and her family, all of whom gave him a warm smile before walking away to return to whatever task was at hand.

The noonday meal had just concluded when Raldus entered the home and approached Ariela as she was clearing the table.

"Why get a new tunic instead of shirts and pants like the men here wear?" she asked him upon noticing his bright white attire cinched tight with a leather belt. When he drew close, she noticed his fresh scent, clear skin, and slick hair from a recent bath.

"I am who I am, and this is more comfortable for me," he replied.

She nodded in understanding and continued with her work.

"Would you join me for a walk?" he requested, causing her to freeze with the last plate halfway up to the shelf.

She glanced at her father, who still sat at the table watching them with a somber smile, and received from him an approving nod. She had been wondering why he hadn't returned to work yet.

"That would be nice," she agreed as she finished putting away the plate. After that, she wiped her hands on a towel, then gave him a quick nod to show she was ready. He led the way through the house, and as she followed, she wondered if she should change into something nicer to match his attire, but he walked so fast that it was all she could do to keep up.

Once outside, Raldus must have realized that he was going too fast because he slowed to a pace more suited for her shorter legs as he headed to the south. Neither spoke as they ascended the stairs to the monastery, crossed the plaza, and exited through the gate.

"Where are we going?" she asked semi-breathless, unable to contain her curiosity any longer.

"It's just a little further," he promised as he turned off the path into the woods. She pulled her dress tight to keep it clear of the bushes and followed, carefully but without fear.

We clearly have different definitions of 'just a little further', she thought as several minutes later they were still making their way along the east wall back to the north. Yet she refrained from complaining and kept following in the path created by his large feet and powerful steps.

At the northeast corner, they made a slight turn to the north and began moving away from the wall. A few minutes later, they finally broke out from the trees to see her pond, her favorite place to be alone and think which she'd shown him all those months ago.

"Please, rest," he suggested with a wave of the hand toward the large, flat rock near the water's edge. She gratefully accepted and looked out over the water, marveling at how different it looked during the day.

The sunlight shone on the brown water, fish jumped at bugs, and on the other side a deer resumed slaking its thirst after determining they weren't a threat. She had only ever been here at night since wandering outside the walls was strictly forbidden except for hunting trips, forcing her to sneak out as a child when she desired to see something new.

That also meant she'd always had to climb over the wall, and the best spot to do that was actually a much shorter route than the one they had just taken, causing her to wonder why he hadn't gone that way. Knowing him, he did it to show the others, and her, that he was still his own man who only followed the rules with which he agreed and was daring anyone to make him do otherwise.

"This is where I first realized that our upbringing and standards are not all that different, and I also learned there is more to you than meets the eye," Raldus mentioned from where he stood to her left after a few minutes had passed.

She looked up at him to see him thoughtfully looking out over the water. Not wanting to interrupt his muse, she chose not to respond, not that there was anything she could say to that anyway.

"You are the reason I'm alive today, in more ways than one. These past months have shown me much, and I find myself thinking about the future in ways that never before even entered my mind," he continued.

"It has been quite a journey," she observed. He met her gaze, then knelt before her, clasping her hands in his. Her breath seized as his green eyes peered deep into her own.

"All my life, I thought I was complete as I was. I neither needed nor wanted anyone else, mortal or immortal. I was wrong. I needed Rosjen, and I want a family. Your father has given me permission to join yours."

Tears welled up in her eyes, but she held them back and waited for him to finish.

"Ariela fret Imri, will you marry me and continue teaching me the way of peace?"

"Yes!" she choked out as the tears flowed, and he pulled her close, wrapping her up in his powerful arms as she buried her face in his neck.

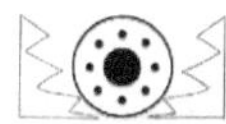

The sun rose over the town, bathing it in a golden glow as Raldus watched from what had become his favorite spot near the blacksmith, which sat to the northwest of the town atop a height. Its warmth was a welcome reprieve from the chilly morning hours and he watched as it slowly rose beyond the forest.

He heard someone approaching from behind, but made no move to look or ready himself.

"You've been coming out here a lot," his wife remarked as she draped a blanket over his shoulders. He took the gray sheet in both hands to keep it in place, but did not pull it in close.

"I expected my heart to be at peace by now, but a burden remains upon it," he explained as she sat on the rocky ground beside him and pulled her red shawl tight.

"Tell me."

"The scriptures say that all of us are called to a purpose according to our gifts. Everyone says that this is the way of peace, but my gifts are for war."

"Is that why you've continued training even after marrying me, moving into my father's house, and working with him and the other farmers?"

"I don't feel right if I don't train. My spirit compels me to keep my skills sharp and remain ready for a fight."

She didn't respond to this and the two of them sat in silence. Below them, people left their homes as the sky brightened, heading to whatever work awaited them.

"Does that mean my faith is untrue?" he finally questioned, and she placed a hand on his knee as she peered into his eyes with a reassuring smile.

"No. I think you're right, and that all of us are called to different purposes. One thing I learned last summer is that wherever peace can be found, evil is never far away, and men like you must fight it if any are to live free," she told him.

He looked deep into her hazel eyes, where he saw a deep wellspring of loving wisdom, and pulled her in close for a passionate kiss.

After they separated, he climbed to his feet, then gave her a hand up and was about to walk with her back to the house when he felt a shiver crawl down his spine. He tensed up and looked back to the east, seeing not the town or forest outside the wall, but rather a memory far beyond his physical sight.

"What is it?" Ariela asked, her voice rising with concern.

"We never did learn who was supporting the bandits," he mused. They'd also never found that man with the staff which shot burning light, but he'd never told her about him and didn't mention it now.

An evil did indeed remain, made even more frightening by the mystery surrounding it. Now he understood he would have to face it again one day.

"No matter. That is of no concern to us now," he concluded, relaxing his posture as he walked away from the precipice.

There was no telling what the future held, but for now, there was only peace and happiness, and that was enough.

Follow the author on Amazon for updates on Book Two!

Acknowledgements

Thank you to my dad for his continued support and encouragement on this never-ending journey of mine.

Special thanks to Maria Secoy and the mentorship team of All Write Well, who gave me the support I needed to complete in a matter of months what otherwise might never have been done.

And to all my friends who tolerate my rambling on about non-existent worlds and my constant requests for feedback.

About the author

An active imagination has been one of Dodge's defining attributes for as long as he can remember, with its creations often seeming more real to him than the world in which he lived. Upon discovering a talent and affinity for the written word, he began writing stories for fun at first, then eventually decided to make it more than a hobby. This has taught him to control his wandering mind while also providing an escape for him and others.

Born in northern Illinois, his family moved to southern Missouri shortly afterward where he currently lives with his two cats Merry and Pippin who provide comfort and drive him crazy multiple times a day. He rides a motorcycle, exercises regularly, and trains in Brazilian Jiu-Jitsu when possible.

Also by Dodge Merrin

Follow me on Amazon!

Rising Shadows Trilogy

Echoes of Darkness

Available through Amazon & KU. https://mybook.to/echoesofdarkness

Night Comes Again

Available through Amazon. https://mybook.to/nightcomesagain

Suffer No Evil

Available through Amazon https://mybook.to/suffernoevil

Embers of Hope Science Fiction Miniseries

Triumphant Empire

Available through Amazon & KU. https://mybook.to/faRL1

Revolution

Available through Amazon. https://mybook.to/cNVFXJ

Total War

Available through Amazon. https://mybook.to/7Ph2

Brink of Extinction

Available through Amazon. https://mybook.to/CeUCF

See Also

Humble Glory

Available through Amazon & KU. https://mybook.to/H4ePYWh

www.ingramcontent.com/pod-product-compliance
Lightning Source LLC
LaVergne TN
LVHW090601110826
845146LV00001B/220

* 9 7 9 8 9 9 0 9 0 7 9 1 1 *